The House Always Wins

By

Shanika Roach

Copyright © 2018 Shanika Roach
Published by Anointed Inspirations Publishing, LLC

Note: This is a work of fiction. Names, characters, places and incidents either are products of the author's imagination or are used fictitiously. Any resemblance to actual events or locales or persons, living or dead, is entirely coincidental

Anointed Inspirations Publishing is currently accepting Urban Christian Fiction, Inspirational Romance, and Young Adult fiction submissions. For consideration, please send manuscripts to
info@aipublishingllc.com
or
anointedinspirationspublishing@gmail.com
www.aipublishingllc.com

CHAPTER 1

Nathan

"I want them out of this house today!" my wife Miranda screamed in my ear and awakened me.

I slowly opened my eyes and looked into my wife's angry face. "Lower your voice before someone hears you, and you know they can't leave today." My sister Sheila and her daughter Shannon came to stay with us last night because Shelia caught her husband cheating.

"I can't take her being here. She has no respect for me and Shannon is a bad influence on Kendra."

"No, she's not you're exaggerating." I said. And plus, our daughter Kendra was no angel, but I wouldn't dare say that to my wife right now because she already looked like she was ready to explode.

"I'm not exaggerating. Shannon hangs out late and do you see how short some of her dresses are?" That is no way for a teenager to dress."

I sighed and sat up in bed. "That's for her mother to worry about, and you are just going to have to deal with it because they're going to be staying with us for a little while and that's that." I said and got out of bed and headed to the bathroom with Miranda right on my heels.

I turned around and faced Miranda. "Look I can't deal with this right now. I have a big surgery today and I need to be focused."

Miranda glared at me and put her hands on her hips. "So that's it you're just going to dismiss me and my feelings because you have a big surgery today?"

"Yes, because you're making a big deal out of nothing. I know you and Sheila don't get along but that's my sister and she's going through a rough time right now and there is plenty of room in this house. Instead of kicking her while she is down you should try being there for her."

Miranda laughed sarcastically. "Like she is going to listen to anything I have to say."

I shook my head and went to turn on the water in our Jacuzzi tub so I could take a shower. I began removing my clothes. After I finished removing them I kissed my wife softly on the lips. When I tried to deepen the kiss, she pulled away. "Don't be like that. You want to join me in the shower?" I asked and reached for her again.

Miranda stepped back. "No, I don't and you have some nerve to think I'm going to shower and have sex with you after you dismissed my feelings. You have time to have sex with me this morning, but you don't have time to listen to how I feel about your sister being here?"

I blew out a frustrated sigh. "You know what, forget it." I said and got in the shower and closed the glass door. Miranda was really trying my patience this morning. I suggested that we should shower together because I knew that would put us both in a relaxing mood and cut the tension but she couldn't even do that. I grabbed the soap and started lathering my body and then I heard the bathroom door slam. I knew Miranda was angry but she would just have to get over it. Family was supposed to help each other out, and I wasn't going to turn my sister away when she needed me.

After I finished my shower I dried myself off and changed into a pair of jeans and a t-shirt. I went downstairs and I could smell something cooking in the kitchen. I walked into the kitchen and saw that my sister was cooking breakfast. "Good morning Shelia."

"Good morning big brother. Is your bourgeoisie wife going to be joining us for breakfast?"

"Be nice Shelia." I said.

"I'll try but it's kind of hard with her giving me the stink face."

"Am I going to have to stay here a referee you guys?"

"Of course not. Go ahead and sit breakfast will be ready in a minute and then I'm going to have to get Shannon up."

"It smells good in here but I'm going to have to pass. I'm just going to grab something to eat on the way to the hospital because I have an important surgery this morning and I want to get to the hospital early to prepare for it."

"Okay, and thanks for letting me and Shannon stay here. I know Miranda is giving you a fit." She said with a smirk.

I smiled and said "I'll see you later," and then I left the kitchen and walked down the hallway and got my briefcase and bag out of the closet. When I turned around Miranda was standing right behind me and she didn't look to happy and I knew that I needed to say something to soothe my wife's anger. "Listen baby, I know you're not happy about Sheila and Shannon being here, but they need me right now. I just need for you to be the bigger person. Shelia made breakfast so just try to be nice to her." I said and then kissed her softy on the lips.

Miranda's expression softened. "I'll try but I'm not making any promises. Good luck on your surgery. I'm going to get the kids up now. They have slept long enough." Miranda said and then walked away.

I left the house and got into my Porsche Cayenne hoping that my wife and sister didn't kill each other.

CHAPTER 2

Nathan

I tried to relax as I drove to St. Allen's Hospital in Phoenix, Arizona where I am the chief of general surgery. I had picked up a sausage biscuit and a order of hash browns from McDonalds and I quickly gobbled it down, and took a huge sip from my cup of orange juice. I turned on the radio hoping the music would help. I was excited and a little nervous to be performing surgery on Stanley Harlow. He is sixty-five and one of the best and well-respected general surgeons all over the country. He is also my mentor. It was an honor to learn from him. But Stanley had gotten bad news a couple of months ago. He found out he had a cancerous tumor on his liver, and he picked me to perform the surgery. It is a risky surgery because the tumor is huge, but I was confident that I could remove the tumor with no problem. Surgery was what I did best, but it was a long road to get here.

My full name is Nathaniel Earl Mills, but everyone calls me Nathan. I grew up in Phoenix, Arizona and I came from a working-class family. My father Reginald was a police officer and my mother Diane was a bank teller. We got by and lived comfortably until my father was killed in the line of duty when I was eleven and my sister was eight. It was devastating to our family. My mother was left alone to raise my sister and I. My father had a life insurance policy but it was only enough to give him a decent burial and pay off some bills. With my father gone my mother took on a second job as a waitress. My mother did her best to take good care of us, she was a Christian woman and raised us with Christian values. She took us to church as much as she

could even if she was tired after working two jobs. As I watched
my mother work hard to take care of us, I knew I had to strive for
excellence. I was always smart and got good grades, but I worked
even harder and when I was in tenth grade I got a grant to attend a
prestigious private school. At first, I didn't want to go to a new
school and leave all my old friends behind, but my mom wouldn't
hear of it. She told me that I had to take this opportunity. So, I
went to the private school with a bunch of rich kids. I felt out of
place at first, but I soon became comfortable there and that's where
I first laid eyes on my wife Miranda. Miranda was the most
beautiful girl I had ever seen. She was light-skinned with blue
eyes and long light brown hair. She was slender. She looked like
a young Vanessa Williams. Miranda is still very beautiful, and she
stands at about 5'7. I wasn't bad looking myself. I was slender
and brown skinned with a low haircut. I look the same now except
I have a little more muscles and a neatly trimmed mustache and
I'm 6'0. Miranda was nice to me and I could tell she liked me
even though she was dating a guy named David at the time. At
first, I didn't think I stood a chance because David came from the
same kind of background as Miranda did. Both of her parents
were congress members and her and his parents owned a lot of
businesses throughout Phoenix. But I could tell that Miranda
really liked me and she thought I was brilliant. After a year of
being friends she dumped David and start going out with me and I
fell head over heels in love with her. I had never met a girl like
her. Her parents didn't like it at first because her parents were
such good friends with David's family, but I eventually won them
over and they loved the fact that I wanted to be a surgeon.
Everything was going great up until I was about to graduate until
something tragic happened. My mom had met a nice man named
Ben at church and they had been dating for two years, but I quickly

learned that all people from church weren't good. My mom and I came home early from shopping and we caught Ben raping my sister. I quickly pulled him off of Shelia who was only fifteen at the time and tried to beat the life out of him, and he had the nerve to say she wanted it. If it wasn't for my mother pulling me off of him, I probably would have killed him. They called the police and Ben was later convicted of rape, but all through the trial he kept saying it was consensual, and the most he could be charged for was statutory rape. But the judge and jury didn't buy his story and my sister's teary account of what happened helped. Ben was convicted of rape and sentenced to fifteen years in prison. When he was released from prison, I heard he left the state, and it was a good thing because I don't know what I would have done to him if I got my hands on him. But after all that my family managed to put the pieces of our lives back together again.

Miranda and I went to college together, but she got pregnant right when I was about to start medical school. Miranda said she wanted to be a doctor as well, but I honestly didn't think that's what she really wanted because she wasn't that passionate about it. I think she just wanted to be a doctor because she thought that was what would make her parents happy. She told me she would stay home with the baby while I went to medical school, and when my son Timothy was born I was so happy, and she got pregnant with Kendra two years later and she was more than happy to stay at home, and she took care of the house and kids as I went on to become a successful surgeon. Later on Miranda started her own foundation to give out scholarships to teenage girls. I bought us a beautiful two-story five-bedroom house. I also brought my mother a house, because it was because of her that I worked so hard to become a surgeon, but three years ago my mother was diagnosed with Alzheimer's. My sister and I were heartbroken when we found out and I offered to have my mother move in with me since I had more room in my house, but my mother's disease progressed rapidly, and Miranda couldn't deal with it because she was the one that had to watch my mother since I was working, so we moved her into a nursing home. I visited her as much as I could.

I am now forty-two and Miranda is forty-one. Miranda and I have a nice life and I tried to be there for my family as much as I could, but being a surgeon was a very demanding job, and I needed for my wife to have my back especially on days like today. She didn't understand that I had to be there for my family. Not everyone was fortunate to grow up the way she did. And I made a vow to myself that I would always be there for my sister and mother because we had it so hard after my father died. Timothy is seventeen and will be graduating from high school this year and Kendra is fifteen. I tied to set a good example for my family. The man was the head of the household and I saw first-hand what can happen to a family when it loses a strong father figure, and I didn't want anything like that to happen to my family. I raised my family as Christians the same as how my mother raised me.

I pulled into St. Allen's hospital and parked in my reserved parking space and got out of the car and entered the hospital. I went to the attending's lounge to change into my scrubs and then I went into Stanley's hospital room where the chief of surgery Alex Simpson was talking to him and his wife.

"Hello there Mr. and Mrs. Harlow." I greeted them.

"Oh, stop with the formalities and call me Stanley like you always do. I don't care if the chief of surgery is here." Stanley said with a laugh and Alex laughed as well.

"I'm going to take very good care of you today." I said. I turned around when the room door opened and my surgical resident Tammy Linden and her intern Sandy Carr walked in.

"Hello, Mr. Harlow." How are you feeling this morning?" Dr. Linden asked.

"I'll feel better once this tumor comes out." Stanley said.

"Well that's the plan." Dr. Linden said.

Dr. Linden and I went over the surgical plan again with Stanley and his wife and then we went to go get prepared for the surgery. As we were scrubbing in (that's what we called it when we were sanitizing before surgeries) Dr. Linden asked. "Are you sure you're ready for this?"

"Of course, he's ready." I turned around and saw Leah walking into the scrubbing area. Leah was my scrub nurse and she always had my back on everything. Leah was very pretty. She was light brown with reddish brown hair that she wore naturally curly and she stood at about 5'3 and she had a nice body. Her scrubs did nothing to hide her full breasts and curvy frame. She is thirty years old.

"Thanks Leah." I said.

"Don't mention it." she said with a smile and started washing her hands.

"I hate to break up this little moment, but this is a very serious surgery we are about to perform." Dr. Linden said.

"Don't you think I know that." I said.

Dr. Linden is an attractive brunette in her late thirties and she is a shark when it comes to surgeries. She's very smart and competitive and she likes to challenge me on everything, and I often had to remind her who was in charge here.

"If anything goes wrong in there it's going to be our butts on the line, and I don't need something like that on my resume."

I shook my head. "Where is your confidence Linden?"

She frowned at me. "Of course, I'm confident." She said.

"Okay then. Let's go perform this surgery." I said and went into the operating room where Stanley was already under anesthesia. Dr. Linden and Leah joined me a moment later. The nurses put on our gloves and surgical aprons. Dr. Linden took her place across from me and Leah stood next to me ready to hand me the surgical instruments I needed. "Scalpel." I said and Leah handed me the scalpel. I closed my eyes and said a quick prayer like I always do before I operate on my patients and then I proceeded with the surgery.

"Wow, look at that tumor." Dr. Linden said in amazement as we took the huge tumor out.

"Yes, it is." I said and then I noticed something else that caught my attention.

"Oh no." I said as I examined his liver further.

"What is it?" Dr. Linden asked and then her mouth went wide in shock. "Please don't tell me that's another tumor."

"It is." I said shaking my head.

"It wasn't there the last time we took an ex-ray of his liver."
Dr. Linden said inspecting the tumor.

The tumor wasn't as big as the first one we removed, but it was sizeable. "How did we miss this?" I asked in frustration. Then as I continued to inspect it I realized that the way it was positioned that the ex-ray couldn't pick it up. It was in a dangerous location. It was close by his hepatic artery, but I knew I could remove it safely. I thought about what to do for a moment and then I said. "I think we should remove it."

"We can't do that because he didn't authorize it, and plus removing that second tumor would kill him. He's been under long enough and his heart may not be able to take that, and if you even nick one of his arteries he will be in major trouble and we will be racing the clock to prepare it." Dr. Linden said.

I thought about everything Dr. Linden was saying, but I didn't want to close him up only to have to remove this tumor later. No need to put him through two surgeries and the way the second tumor was positioned and growing he would have less than a year to live. "I think we should remove it now because we are just going to have to do it again later anyway."

"I know but waiting will give his body time to heal before a second surgery." Dr. Linden debated.

"I disagree. I'm going to talk to his wife." I said and removed my surgical gloves and exited out of the operating room and down the hall to the waiting room. When his wife saw me, she stood up anxiously.

"How did it go?" she asked nervously

"It went well we removed the tumor with no problem, but we saw another tumor growing on his liver." I said

"Another tumor? How can that be?" his wife questioned.

"The tumor was positioned in a way that wouldn't show up on a normal ex-ray. You have a couple of options. I could close him up and we can schedule to remove the tumor at a later date or I can go ahead and remove it now, and it can save Stanley from having to go through a whole other surgery."

His wife gave me a conflicted look and I could tell that she was torn about what to do. "What do you think I should do?" she asked.

"I can't tell you what to do, but I would recommend that we go ahead and remove it. It will be risky because the tumor is close by one of his arteries, but I think that's the best option."

She nodded her head. "Stanley trusted you and he always said you were great so if you think it would be best to do it then I say do it."

"Okay, I will do everything in my power to make sure he's okay." I said.

"Okay." She said, and a tear slid down her cheek.
I knew this was hard and scary for her and that just made me want to work even harder to make sure that the surgery was successful.

I left the waiting room and went back to the operating room. I sanitized my hands again and then went quickly over to Stanley. The nurse put a fresh pair of gloves on my hands. "Stanley's wife gave me permission to remove the second tumor so lets get started."

"You're making a mistake." Dr. Linden complained.

I could feel my temper start to rise. "If you disagree with my decision you can leave, and I can get another resident to take your place." I said firmly

"Of course, I'm not going to leave, but I wouldn't be a good resident if I didn't give you my honest opinion."

"Whatever let's get started." As soon as I removed the tumor with Dr. Linden's assistant the machine's started beating loudly and blood started to fill up around his liver.

"He's BP is going up. We have to find the source of this bleed." Dr. Linden's said frantically

As I was trying to find the source of the bleed, I realized that his hepatic artery had burst and I knew we were in trouble. How did that happen? I was so careful Dr. Linden and I tried desperately to try to repair the artery, but he flatlined. After he flatlined, I refused to give up and I instructed Dr. Linden to shock his heart twice when that didn't work I began to perform chest compressions. I worked frantically for fifteen minutes but Dr. Linden looked me with a defeated expression.

"Mills you've been at this for fifteen minutes you need to call it." she said.

"No, I can't call it. I told his wife I could do this."

"He's gone." Dr. Linden said.

I was overcome with a deep feeling of remorse and I knew I had messed up in a big way. This was over, and he wasn't coming back. There was no need to prolong this any further. I looked at the clock. "Time of death 10:21."

CHAPTER 3

Miranda

After Nathan left this morning, I was dreading to have to interact with his sister. It was nice of her to cook breakfast this morning, but then she had to make snide remarks about how I should have been the one up cooking breakfast since I didn't have a real job. I ran a charity that gave out scholarships to teenage girls, but she didn't think that was real work. Shelia had a job as a legal secretary at a law firm and she made good money and her husband Darryl worked as a carpenter. So together they were able to live comfortably. Both of their salaries combined couldn't touch Nathan's two million dollars a year salary as the general surgery chief at the hospital. I kept my cool because I promised Nathan that I would try to get along with his sister, but she had to remember that she was living in my house and she needed to be respectful. I managed to get through breakfast without arguing with her.

I was home alone, and I was glad for the moment. I didn't have to work at my organization today, so I planned to go to the gym later. But to be honest I didn't work at the organization much. I hired my best friend Crystal and she basically ran it for me. I was just about to head into the den to watch TV when the phone rang. I went to answer it.

"Hello, may I speak to Mr. or Mrs. Mills."

"This is Mrs. Mills." I said wondering what this call was about.

"Mrs. Mills this is Principal Warner and I'm calling to let you know that your daughter Kendra was caught smoking marijuana in the girls' bathroom." He informed me.

"That must be some kind of mistake because my daughter doesn't smoke marijuana." I said in shock.

"I assure you that this was not a mistake. I need you to come pick-up Kendra from school because she is expelled."

"Sure thing." I said feeling my anger start to rise. I ended the call with Principal Warner and quickly sprinted upstairs to grab my purse and car keys. Once I retrieved them I left the house and jumped into my Mercedes and headed to the school in a hurry.

"I can't believe that girl." I said out loud. Kendra had always given Nathan and me trouble. Either she was staying out late or sneaking in clubs that she wasn't supposed to go to. Kendra and Tim both went to Gaston Academy, a prestigious private school. Kendra had gotten caught skipping classes a few times, and the reason why she wasn't kicked out of school is because Principal Warner is a close friend of my father's. My father is the former Mayor of Phoenix and he has a lot of friends in high places. Kendra was the splitting image of me and I was happy to have a daughter that resembled me so much but some of her actions lately were really starting to concern me. While Kendra is rebellious Tim is the total opposite. He is very smart, well-behaved and focused. Tim got accepted into Princeton, Stanford and, a lot of other prestigious Ivy League colleges. But Tim was leaning towards Princeton but I really hoped that he would choose Stanford because it was closer. I was so proud of Tim he was so much like his father and he looked like him as well. They were the same height and complexion. Tim inherited my blue eyes though. That was one of the main reasons why I fell in love with Nathan. I never met a man more focused and driven then him.

When I arrived at the school I went inside and headed towards the principal office. The secretary told me I could go ahead to his office. I knocked on the door and the principal told me to come right in. When I walked inside Kendra was sitting down with a defiant look on her face and I could feel my blood start to boil. She could at least look apologetic, but no she was sitting there like she had somewhere better to be.

"Hello, I'm sorry we had to meet like this again." Principal Warner said.

"So am I." I said and glared at Kendra.

"As I told you before Kendra will be expelled from school for five days."

"Five days? Her grades are already poor. Can I come to the school and pick-up her assignments from her teachers, because I don't want her to fall too far behind in her school work?" I said.

"I know, but five days is lenient. It should be ten days, but since I've known you since you were a little girl I will be go easy on Kendra, and it's fine if you pick up her assignments from her teachers."

I looked at Kendra. "What do you have to say for yourself young lady?" I asked.

Kendra shrugged her shoulders. "Can we go home now? I don't feel so good."

"It's probably because of all that marijuana you've been smoking." I turned toward Principal Warner. "Thanks for everything and I assure you that Kendra's behavior and grades will improve. Come on young lady." I ordered and stood up.

Kendra got up and we left the Principal office and as soon as we got inside my car I went off. "I can't believe you. I know you've been doing sneaky things, but since when have you started using drugs?"

"Mom, it's not a big deal. A lot of kids smoke marijuana." Kendra said.

"I don't care what other kids do. I don't want you doing it, now where did you get it?"

Kendra was silent.

"It was Shannon wasn't it."

"No, it wasn't, and you can't keep blaming her for everything."

I turned around and reached in the backseat and picked up Kendra's backpack and started searching through it.

"What are you doing, mom?"

"What does it look like I'm doing. I'm checking your backpack for drugs."

"You can't be serious." Kendra said clearly frustrated.

I ignored her and after I finished searching her backpack I reached down on the passenger side floor and picked up her purse and started going through it.

"You can't go through my purse!" Kendra yelled and tried to yank her purse out of my hand.

"Kendra, you better let go of this purse now! I can go through your purse or anything else I want to." I said as I glared at her.

Kendra stared at me for a moment and when she saw that I meant business she reluctantly let her purse go.

"This just isn't fair." Kendra mumbled.

"It's not fair that I have a daughter that wants to use drugs." I said as I searched through her purse. I opened up a zipper compartment in her purse and saw three condoms. I gasped and pulled them out for Kendra to see.

Kendra eyes went wide. "Not only are you using drugs, but you are having sex too."

"I'm not having sex." Kendra said but she couldn't look me in the eye.

I knew she was lying. "Kendra, I prefer for you to wait until you get married to have sex, but if you are having sex I'm glad you are protecting yourself. But if you claim you are not having sex then why do you have condoms in your purse?"

"A nurse came to our school and talked to us about safe sex and she passed out condoms to the whole class."

Her story sounded believable but something told me she was lying. It bothered me that she was probably having sex, but I was more concerned about her smoking weed. I put the condoms back in her purse and handed it to her, and I put her backpack back in the backseat. I shook my head and started my car and drove out of the parking lot and out on the highway. I didn't believe one word of what Kendra was saying especially about Shannon. It was Shannon who gave her the idea to sneak in that night club, and since then she's been acting out.

"Don't lie to me. I know it was her." I continued my accusations against Shannon

"It wasn't her mom."

"Okay, if it wasn't her then who was it?"

Kendra was silent. Exactly what I thought. The rest of the ride home was silent and when we got inside of the house I laid into Kendra again. "I want you to go upstairs to your room and do you school work because your grades are poor enough as it is."

"Everybody can't get straight A's like Tim."

"I'm not asking you to get straight A's. But you can do a lot better than C's and D's."

"It's the best I can do." Kendra said.

"I don't believe that at all. Tim does so well in school because he applies himself and he works very hard."

Kendra rolled her eyes. "Why are you always comparing me to your golden boy? I'm not perfect like Tim."

I stared at Kendra for a moment. I was a little taken aback by what she said but I was not surprised. She always accused me and Nathan of loving Tim more and treating him better than her, but that wasn't true. We were harder on her because we had to be. "No one is comparing you to Tim and I never said he was perfect."

"Well you sure act like it. Can I go to my room now?"

"Yeah go ahead and I'm about to head out." I said.

Kendra raised her eyebrow. "Where are you going?"

"Don't worry about it. You just get started on your school work." I said and left the house and climbed into my car and pulled off.

I was headed to Shelia's job. It was time that we had a talk about her daughter.

CHAPTER 4

Nathan

"I don't understand. You told me that you could remove his tumor successfully."

"I did remove it successfully, but one of his arteries burst and we couldn't repair it. We tried everything we could, but Stanley died."

"No!" Stanley's wife yelled, and she began crying uncontrollably.

I felt my heart breaking as well. I couldn't believe my former mentor was dead and it was all my fault."

"There is a grief counselor available to talk to you if that's what you need." Dr. Linden told her.

Stanley's wife wiped her tears and pointed her finger at me. "It's all you fault for talking me into that surgery. I shouldn't have listened to you, but I trusted you because Stanley did. And you let him down in a big way. I'm going to sue you and this hospital if I have to!" She yelled attracting the attention of everyone around us.

At that moment, I wished that I could disappear. A couple of nurses came over and pulled her away. I couldn't take it anymore and I turned around and started to walk away.

"You see what you've caused?" Dr. Linden asked as she appeared beside me.

"Not now Linden. I need to think."

"You are so arrogant. You knew how risky removing that tumor was, but you just had to go ahead and do it anyway. Now Mrs. Harlow is talking about suing us.

I stopped walking and faced her. "Is that what you're so concerned about, getting sued? Well you don't need to worry because she said she was going to sue me and I planned on taking the fall for this anyway."

"Good because it was you fault." Dr. Linden said and walked away.

I couldn't believe that woman. I knew how cold she was, but I thought she could at least muster a little support in a situation like this. I walked to the attending's lounge and no sooner than I sat down I got a page. It was from the chief of surgery and I knew I was in big trouble.

There was no need to prolong the inevitable, so I walked to his office feeling like an inmate about to be led to execution. Once I arrived at his office I knocked on his door.

"Come in." he said

I slowly opened the door and walked inside. Chief Simpson was sitting in the leather chair behind his desk and he didn't look to happy at all. I sat down in the chair across from him.

"Betty Harlow just left my office and she informed me that she is going to come back with her lawyers because she is suing you and maybe this hospital because she said you talked her into a risky surgery that killed her husband. Now what happened in that operating room?" Chief Simpson asked.

I told him everything that happened during the surgery. After I finished telling him Chief Simpson shook his head and looked at me with disappointment.

"You should have never talked her into removing that second tumor, but that artery was in danger of rupturing anyway from the pressure of that tumor. It was only a matter of time before it ruptured so this isn't your fault."

I put my face in my hands and I felt like I was going to break down.

"Don't be too hard on yourself Mills, but the fact that you talked her into the surgery and then he died makes you and this hospital look bad. Once everyone finds out what happened to Stanley people will start to question everything about this hospital. I'll try to talk to Betty again once she's calmed down some. I don't think she will win the case, but it will bring a lot of negative attention to this hospital."

"Maybe I can talk to her and explain everything to her again. I could have explained things better to her but it was hard for me because I was still in shock myself." I offered.

"No, you will not talk to her. I shouldn't even talk to her, but I'm going to try anyway. Meanwhile I want you to get me all the paper work from this surgery."

"Okay." I said and stood up.

"Do you have any more surgeries today?" Chief Simpson asked.

"Yes, I have to remove a gallbladder in a couple of hours."

"Are you okay to operate?"

"Yes. Removing a gallbladder is a simple surgery. I could do that with my eyes closed."

Chief Simpson studied me for a moment and then said okay.

I left his office and told one of the interns to get up all the paperwork from Stanley Harlow's surgery and take it to chief's office and then I walked to the attending's lounge. I got comfortable on the couch and when I looked up Leah was standing in the doorway.

"Are you okay?" she asked.

I shrugged my shoulders. "I'm going to try to be." I said.

Leah walked into the room and sat down on the couch next to me. "What happened in that operating room was not your fault. You did what you thought was best and it doesn't matter what Dr. Linden or anyone else says." Leah said

"Thanks for that, but I really shouldn't have pushed her to let me remove that second tumor."

Leah stared into my eyes. "You need to go out and get this off your mind. Do you want to go out with me tonight? I know this nice bar we could go to. They have drinks and gambling. That would take your mind off it for sure."

I couldn't deny I was attracted to Leah and I know she liked me because she flirted with me a lot, but I knew going out with her would be wrong. "I appreciate the offer, but I can't and plus I don't drink and gamble."

Leah gave me a flirtatious smile. "I know you're married, but it wouldn't hurt for us to hang out together and they have high stakes poker games every night and I don't know a man that doesn't know how to play poker."

I couldn't help but smile. "I do know how to play poker, but I really can't go out with you."

"Okay, but give me your cell phone. I'm going to put in my cell phone number in case you change your mind." She said.

Even though I knew I shouldn't I removed my cell phone from my pocket and handed it to her and I watched as she typed her number into my cell phone. After she typed it in she handed me back my phone and stood up.

"I'll be expecting your call." She said and winked at me and left the lounge.

After she left I sat there for a moment contemplating her offer. She had managed to temporarily take my mind off what had happened and lift my spirits a little after only being around her for a few minutes so I could only imagine how much joy she could bring me if I went out with her.

CHAPTER 5

Miranda

"I need to see Shelia Washington please." I told the receptionist at the law firm Shelia worked at.

"Mrs. Washington is in the office with Mr. Riles. They are working on a very important case and Mr. Riles said they are not to be disturbed."

"This is very important. I need for you to interrupt them and I'm not leaving here until I talk to Mrs. Washington." I said firmly. I didn't care how important their case was this was more urgent at the moment.

The receptionist hesitated for a moment then said. "You can have a seat on the couch and I'll go see if I can get Mrs. Washington for you."

"Thank you." I said and went and sat on the couch.

The receptionist got up and walked around the corner. She came back a few minutes later and said. "She will come to see you in a few minutes.

I nodded my head. About fifteen minutes Shelia came marching around the corner. Shelia is a very attractive woman. She is brown-skinned with shoulder length hair and killer curves. She had on a nice skirt and blouse, but in my opinion the skirt was much too short and tight and her cleavage was busting out of her silk V-neck blouse. I could see why her daughter dressed the way she did.

When Shelia arrived in front of me she sat down beside me. "This better be good Miranda."

"Actually, it's not good."

"Wait a minute." Shelia said interrupting me. "Let's go around the corner to the break room where we can have some privacy."

We got up and I followed Shelia down the hall and around the corner to the break room. Once inside we sat down at the round table.

"So, what's not good?" Shelia asked me.

"Kendra was suspended from school for smoking marijuana and I think your daughter gave it her."

"My daughter doesn't smoke weed, so you better check with one of your daughter's preppy friends at that private school she attends."

"I don't need to check with them, because I have a feeling it was your daughter."

"I don't care what kind of feeling you have, it wasn't my daughter. You've been blaming Shannon for everything ever since she got Kendra to sneak into that club. You need to get over it. Kids do things like that. Shannon has been punished for that and she hasn't been in trouble since. So, you're not going to blame my daughter for this." Shelia said angrily.

I thought for a moment. Shelia seemed adamant that Shannon didn't give Kendra the marijuana but I wasn't so sure.

"What's wrong cat got your tongue? I can't believe you have the audacity to come to my job and excuse my daughter of something she didn't do. You are a real piece of work Miranda. I think you know it wasn't Shannon, but you're trying to use anything you can think of to get us out of your house, but guess what Nathan said I can stay as long as I want and that's what I plan to do."

"You know what something doesn't make sense about all of this." I said.

"What doesn't make sense?" Shelia asked in a bored tone.

"If you caught your husband cheating why didn't you kick him out of the house? That's what I would have done. There is no way I would leave my own house when my husband was in the wrong."

"This isn't about you Miranda, and I don't owe you an explanation. But I will humor you. For your information, I left the house because I didn't want to be in the house or sleep in the same bed that my husband had another woman in."

"Okay, well do you plan on finding an apartment or something?"

Shelia rolled her eyes at me. Miranda, you live in a big five-bedroom house. You don't even have to see me that much."

"That's not the point. You should want to get your own place instead of living off your brother."

"You act like I'm some bum from off the street. I'm family and I have a job and I can contribute to your household."

"But you know that Nathan won't take your money." I pointed out.

"What is the real issue here?" Shelia asked and looked at me intently.

I thought about what she said. Shelia and I didn't get along and Shannon was a bad influence on Kendra and I didn't want them living in my home for too long, but if I told her that it would only lead to more arguing. "Just find a place soon." I said and stood up.

"I'll find a place when I find a place, and don't ever come to my job again with this foolishness."

"Have a good rest of your day." I said and gave Shelia a phony smile and left.

As I got in my car and headed home, I was overcome with a sense of dread. I knew Shelia was going to tell Nathan that I came by her job and I knew that she was going to put her own spin on what happened. Shelia was sneaky, and Nathan couldn't see it because he was so hung up on always being there for her since his father died and the rape she went through, but I felt there was more to Shelia's rape story. I tried to mention that to Nathan once and he bit my head off and I vowed to myself that I would never bring it up again. I felt like I had a valid reason for coming to her job, but I knew Nathan wouldn't see it that way. He would take Shelia's side like he always did.

CHAPTER 6

Nathan

I was driving home from the hospital and I was thinking about everything that had occurred today. I was still in shock. This was all new to me. I was used to succeeding in anything I put my mind to, but I failed at this. I've lost patients before, but it was usually something out of my control, but I felt like I could have controlled this. I managed to get through the rest of my surgeries for the day, but they were simple surgeries. After my day ended, I went into the attending's lounge and prayed to God and asked him for direction. I didn't understand how this could happen, but I didn't get an answer from God, but I felt some peace afterwards.

When I arrived home, I pulled in the drive-way and just sat there for a minute. I needed to get my thoughts together. I just wanted to go inside and have a nice dinner with my family and maybe relax and watch TV, but I was sure that Miranda would have other ideas. I knew she was going to start complaining the moment I stepped foot inside the house and I really didn't want to hear all that.

After sitting there for a moment, I got out of the car and went into my house with my work bag hanging from my shoulder. As I was walking through the living room and towards the stairs Shannon and Kendra came out of the kitchen with a big bowl of popcorn and sodas.

"Hey girls." I greeted them.

"Hey dad." Kendra greeted me.

"Hey." Shannon greeted me.

"Have you guys eaten dinner yet?" I asked them.

"Yes, mom ordered a pizza. We were just about to watch a movie." Kendra told me.

"Okay." I said and walked into the kitchen to see if there was any food left.

There were two empty pizza boxes on the kitchen island and I sighed. I was looking forward to a home cooked meal, but I was disappointed that they didn't leave me any pizza. I was about to go upstairs to my bedroom when Shelia walked into the kitchen.

"I'm so glad you're home. Did you know your wife came to my job and accused Shannon of giving Kendra marijuana?"

"Wait a minute Kendra had marijuana?" I asked in shock and I knew my chances of having a relaxing evening just went out the window.

"Apparently so, and Miranda blamed my daughter like she always does, and not only did she accuse my daughter of doing something she didn't do, but she had the nerve to tell me that I needed to hurry up and get out of her house."

"Well don't you worry about that. You can stay with us as long as you need to." I said and sprinted upstairs to my bedroom and sat my work bag by the foot of the bed. Miranda was sitting on our king-sized bed in her light pink silk nightgown.

"Honey, I'm so glad you're home. You wouldn't believe the day I've had."

"What's this I hear about Kendra having marijuana?"

Miranda looked taken aback for a moment but then she said. "Shelia already told you, huh?"

"Yes, she did. Now tell me what happened?"

"Kendra was suspended for five days for smoking marijuana in the bathroom at school."

I shook my head. "We really need to talk some sense into Kendra because she's getting out of control."

"I know, but we need to eliminate the bad influences that she has around her." Miranda said.

"You were wrong for going to Shelia's job to accuse Shannon of giving Kendra marijuana. You have no proof that Shannon gave Kendra that marijuana, unless Kendra told you that, did she?"

Miranda put her head down and I knew that meant no. "Okay then, you need to leave it alone. And I thought you told me you were going to try to get along with Sheila."

"I was until that incident."

"Hey dad, can I go to a movie with Brandy tonight?"

I turned around and saw Tim standing in our doorway. He was dressed in blue jeans and a blue designer shirt, and I could smell cologne on him. I chuckled. "It looks like you are already dressed to go." I said.

Tim laughed. "Well I wanted to be ready just in case you said yes."

"You finished your homework?"

"Of course." Tim replied.

"Well I don't' see why not?" I said.

"Thanks dad. I love you guys." He said and quickly walked away.

I turned around to face my wife. "Tim really likes Brandy." Miranda said.

"I know. She's such a nice girl and she's good for him."

"I know, but I want to make sure he stays focused on his school work."

"He will. I'm going to take my shower now and then we can finish talking about Kendra." I said and went into the bathroom that was connected to the bedroom.

I stripped out of my clothes and took a nice long hot shower. My body and mind was tired and my mind was all over the place. The shower helped me to relax. After showering I dried off and went into the bedroom and changed into my pajama pants and t-shirt and joined my wife on the bed. I really wanted to talk about what happened with Stanley but I knew I needed to talk to my daughter first.

"Please go get Kendra so we can talk to her." I instructed my wife.

Miranda put on her robe and left the bedroom. She returned a few minutes later with Kendra who look like she had an attitude.

"Do we have to do this now? I was watching the best part of the movie." Kendra complained.

"You're lucky we're letting you watch TV at all." Now why were you smoking marijuana in school?" I asked

Kendra shrugged her shoulders. "I just wanted to try it." she responded.

"So, that was your first time smoking it?" I asked.

"Yes." Kendra said.

"I don't believe that for a second. You and Shannon have probably been smoking for a while."

"Miranda, I told you to stop accusing Shannon."

"She better if she knows what's good for her." Shelia said appearing in our doorway and I knew things were about to get really bad.

"What are you doing listening in on our conversation. We're having a private family moment." Miranda said loudly.

"I wasn't trying to listen I just happened to be walking by and I have a right to defend my daughter when she has been wrongly accused of something." Shelia said getting in my wife's face.

I quickly jumped out of bed and stepped between them. "Okay calm down you two. Miranda Kendra already told you that Shannon didn't give her the marijuana so why are keep insisting that she did?" I asked and I could feel myself getting angry with my wife. Why couldn't she leave Shannon out of this?

"Because she won't tell me who gave it to her, and it has to be because she's covering for Shannon."

"That does it!" Sheila yelled and tried to reach around me to grab Miranda, but I quickly held her back and guided her out of the room and we walked downstairs and into the kitchen. "You see what I mean? You wife is evil. I don't know why she keeps blaming Shannon for this."

Shannon walked into the kitchen. "Is Aunt Miranda still blaming me for Kendra getting caught smoking?"

That made me even angrier with Miranda. She had no right to blame Shannon. "Don't worry about it Shannon I know you didn't do anything wrong. I will handle Miranda. She won't be blaming you anymore." I said, and I meant it. I wasn't going to tolerate Miranda's behavior toward them anymore.

Shannon nodded her head and went into the refrigerator and got another soda and then she left the kitchen.

Shelia shook her head. "I'm telling you I can't take too much more of this, and she had the nerve to show up at my job with this."

"It's going to be alright. You are welcome here as long as you want to stay, and I don't want Shannon to feel unwelcome?"

"Thanks, big brother." Shelia said and she walked over to me and gave me a hug.

"You're welcome, but I have to ask you if you've tried to talk to Darryl."

"I can't right now." Shelia said and put her head down."

"I understand, but I thought he would at least try to stop by here or something." I said. I didn't understand why Darryl wasn't trying harder to get his family back.

Shelia shrugged her shoulders. "Maybe he is too busy with his new woman."

"I know this is hard for you and I'm here for you." I said.

"I appreciate that." Shelia said.

"Anytime." I said and then I went upstairs to our room where I heard Miranda fussing with Kendra. "Stop it you two. Kendra, you can go downstairs and finish watching the movie with Shannon. We'll talk to you tomorrow. I need to talk to your mother."

Kendra quickly left the room.

"Why did you do that? We need to talk to her."

"Listen I don't like your attitude towards my family, and I don't want you hurting Shannon's feelings with your accusations. I believe she's telling the truth."

"Please." Miranda said and smacked her lips.

I stared at my wife and I didn't like how cold she was acting. How would she feel if someone was accusing Kendra like this? I no longer wanted to be in her presence and I went into our walk-in closet and began to change clothes. Miranda followed behind me.

"Where are you going? We haven't finish talking yet." She said with an exasperated look on her face.

"Well I'm done talking tonight and I'm going out."

"Where are you going?"

"Don't worry about it." I said and put on my shoes and brushed passed her. I went into my work bag and took my keys out and left the bedroom with Miranda on my heels.

"You better tell me where you're going!" she shouted at me.

I ignored her and walked out the door and got into my Porsche and left. I didn't feel like dealing with Miranda tonight. She was constantly worrying about herself and she didn't once ask me how my day went or how my big surgery went today. I knew she was worried about Kendra but she could have still mentioned it.

I pulled out my phone and pulled up Leah's number and dialed it. She answered on the third ring. "Text me your address. I'm going to take you up on your offer." I said to her.

CHAPTER 7

Nathan

Leah was happy to hear from me and she texted me her address. I pulled up to the nice condominium complex. I walked out and waited to get buzzed in and then I took the elevator to the third floor where her condo was located. When I arrived on the floor I found her apartment number and knocked on the door.

Leah opened the door with a big smile on her face. "Hello there, come right on in." she said and stepped aside so I could enter the condo.

I walked inside and was impressed with her condo. It was beautifully furnished and decorated nicely.

"You can have a seat. I have to finish getting dressed. You can watch TV if you want to. I will be right back." She said and went upstairs.

I sat back and relaxed. I picked up the remote control that was sitting on the coffee table and hit the power button to the fifty-five-inch flat screen TV. I turned the channel to CNN because I liked to keep up with what was going on in the world. My cell phone rang, and I pulled it out of my pocket and looked at the screen. It was Miranda and I sent her to voicemail. Leah returned about twenty minutes later and when I saw her my mouth went wide in shock. She was dressed in blue tight-fitting jeans and a nice lavender blouse. She had a medium sized purse on her shoulder. Her curves were amazing. I was not used to seeing look like this because I only saw her in her nurse's scrubs.

"Wow, you look amazing." I said.

"Thank you. I was hoping you would like it. Are you ready, because you looked pretty comfortable sitting on the couch."

I stood up. "I was comfortable but I'm ready to go now." I said looking her up and down. I couldn't help myself.

Leah grinned and started walking towards the door with me following behind her. We left out of the condo and headed towards my Porsche. She gave me directions to the bar. I pulled into the parking lot of Murphy's Bar and Lounge. It was a nice sized establishment and I immediately noticed a bunch of motorcycles parked in the front.

"What's up with the motorcycles?" I asked her.

"Oh, the guys that runs the place are part of a motorcycle club and they are also loan sharks. Most of them are Irish."

"That's interesting." I said, and we got out of the car. As we were walking towards the double doors I felt a little uneasy.

"It's okay, just relax." Leah said and gently squeezed my arm. I opened the door and held it as Leah walked in first.

I followed behind her. There was music playing and people sitting at the bar drinking and laughing. There were also people sitting at tables eating and conversing and as we walked further inside I saw there were slot machines, crap tables, and four people had a game of pool going.

"Come on, let's go around the corner. This is where I have the most fun." Leah told me and she guided me around the corner and into a large room. Four people were sitting around the table playing what looked like a game of poker. We sat in the chairs that was around the table.

"We want to play in the next game, Harry." Leah said to the large middle-age bald man seated at the table."

"Sure, thing Leah, and I see you brought a friend with you."

"Yes, I did." Leah said and looked at me and smiled.

We waited another ten minutes for them to finish the game and then two of the players left and me and Leah joined Harry and a white woman in her mid-thirties.

"Glad you could join us." Harry said

"Thanks." I said.

"This is a high-stakes poker game." Harry informed me.

"How high?" I asked.

"We going to start betting at fifty-dollars and we will keep going up. We have an ATM machine in the front just in case you run out of money." Harry said.

I had about three hundred dollars in my wallet. If I needed more I would just get it. Harry dealt the cards and we began to play poker. As we played we made small talk and I learned that Harry Murphy was one of the owners. He owned it along with his two other brothers and the woman Joan that was sitting with him was his wife. Harry was impressed to know that I was a surgeon. My cell phone rang and I pulled it out of my pocket and turned it off without seeing who was calling because I knew it was my wife and I didn't want to talk to her. I just wanted to enjoy my time out. I had two queens in my hand and two jacks in my hand and I was hoping I would get another queen. Harry raised the pot to one hundred dollars and I was confident I would get another queen or at least another jack so I raised the pot to two hundred dollars. There was five hundred dollars in the pot. Harry raised the pot another five hundred dollars and the pot was now at a thousand dollars. Joan and Leah folded, and it was now my move. I thought for a second. If Harry doubled the pot he had to have an excellent hand, but I was still confident as well, so I matched the bet, I told him I needed to hit the ATM, but I was good for it. I picked another card and got the queen I was hoping for. I wanted to smile but I kept my poker face.

Harry put down his cards. "Three Kings." He said confidently.

I grinned and then laid my cards on the table a full house. I had three queens and two jacks, so I won.

Harry shook his head. "You got this one Doc." He said.

I raked the money my way and looked at Leah and winked. She gave me a big smile. I felt this immediate rush. I had been feeling so down about the failed surgery and about the mini war going on at my house, but now I felt good and confident. And I knew I had just found something amazing to do in my down time.

I excused myself from the table and went to the ATM machine and withdrew two thousand dollars and returned to the table. The waitress came over to the table and brought us food and drinks. I normally didn't drink but I was enjoying myself so much I decided to indulge. We played a few more games and when it was all said and done I had won five thousand dollars and I was on an incredible high.

"We have to do this again soon Doc. You were lucky tonight but I'm sure I will get you next time." Harry said and chuckled.

"Yes, we will definitely do this again." Leah and I left out of the room.

"I'm going to call us a cab to take us back to my place since we both have been drinking." Leah suggested.

"That's a good idea, but how am I supposed to get home and explain all this to my wife?" I asked finally thinking about Miranda.

"Don't worry about all that." Leah said seductively and kissed me on the cheek.

I stared into her eyes and I was exactly where I wanted to be at the moment. When the cab arrived, the driver drove us back to Leah's place and I paid him. We went inside Leah's place and she turned on the lights.

"Have a seat on the couch. I'll be right back." Leah said.

I sat on the couch like she instructed and she returned about fifteen minutes later and stood in front of me wearing red lingerie that put her amazing body on display. No words needed to be said I stood up and kissed her passionately and had my hands all over her soft body. I never cheated on Miranda before, but I had to have Leah. Leah broke the kiss and took my hand and led me upstairs to her bedroom where we had explosive sex.

CHAPTER 8

Miranda

The next morning, I was in the kitchen making breakfast for Kendra and I, but my mind was on Nathan. I couldn't believe that he didn't come home last night and on top of that he wasn't answering his phone. It was bad enough that he humiliated me last night by walking out on me the way he did. Shelia couldn't wait to after Nathan left to rub in the fact that Nathan will always be there for her regardless of what I had to say, and she said she didn't blame Nathan for leaving last night. The nerve of her. I would think that she would have a little more compassion. I mean she did catch her husband cheating with another woman, so she shouldn't want to try to stir up trouble in my house.

"It smells good in here." Kendra said.

I turned around to look at my daughter who was dressed in jeans and a shirt. "It will be ready in a few minutes." I made French toast, turkey bacon, and grits. I fixed our plates while Kendra poured us glasses of orange juice, and we both sat down at the table. Tim and Shannon had already left for school and Sheila was at work.

"So, dad still isn't home, huh." Kendra said as she took a bite of her French toast.

"No, he isn't, but you shouldn't concern yourself with that because we still didn't get a chance to talk to you." I said.

"Are you going to tell him about the condoms you found?" Kendra asked.

I thought about it. We had enough to talk about concerning Kendra, so I decided I would shelf the conversation about the condoms. "No, I won't, but you have to promise me you won't smoke anymore marijuana and pull up your grades. How are you supposed to get into a good college with those grades?"

Kendra sighed. "I honestly don't think college is for me."

I gave her a stern look. "Well you better change your way of thinking, and you better not let your father hear you talking like that."

"I'm just being honest." Kendra said.

I didn't say anything further on the subject and we finished our breakfast in silence. Kendra put the dishes in the dishwasher and I told her I was going to stop by the gym for a little while. And I told Kendra to make sure she started on her school work. I needed to work off some of this stress. I still couldn't believe that Nathan walked out on me the way he did. I mean maybe I was wrong for blaming Shannon, but he still should have had my back. I was his wife after all. I was supposed to come first, not his sister and her drama.

After I finished working out at the gym, I took a shower in one of the bathrooms and I put on some fresh clothes and decided to do some grocery shopping. I was on the cereal aisle when I heard someone call my name.

I turned around and was shocked to see David James my ex-boyfriend. He was still handsome. David is light-skinned with wavy hair that he wears in a close haircut. He stands at about 5'10 and has a medium build.

"It's good to see you Miranda. You're looking better than ever. It looks like life has been good to you." David said looking me up and down.

"It's good to see you too, and you look good as well. Are you visiting?" I asked because the last I heard he was living in California.

"No actually I'm back in Arizona now. I've been here for about six months now. My wife and I just divorced, and I decided to move back closer to home."

"Sorry to hear that. What are you up to now?"

"I'm a real estate developer now."

"Wow, that's good." It was nice to see that he was doing well for himself. I had broken up with him because Nathan had so much more drive and focus while David wasn't as driven and had no real dreams and aspirations.

"I would love to take you out and tell you all that I have been up to."

I had to admit I was curious about what he had been up to but I knew I couldn't. "I'm sorry I can't."

"Why because of Nathan? I know you two are married, but I just wanted to catch up with you."

I hesitated a moment then said. "I really shouldn't."

David smiled. "I understand but I can tell you want to. I'll tell you what, I will give you my number and you can give me a call if you change your mind."

We exchanged numbers and then David left the aisle. I finished grocery shopping with David heavily on my mind. After I paid for my items, I got in my car and headed home. Seeing him brought up so many old feelings but I knew I needed to bury them because I had a lot of things to deal with and I didn't have much time left over to think about him.

CHAPTER 9

Nathan

I woke up groggy and looked around and for a moment I didn't know where I was until I looked beside me and saw Leah sleeping peacefully beside me. Then everything came flooding back to me. While I had an amazing time last night reality started to sink in and I knew I was going to have some explaining to do. I quickly hopped out of bed awakening Leah.

"Good morning sexy, you're rushing off I see."

"Yeah, I have to shower and take a cab to the Lounge and Bar to get my car."

"Yeah, I understand and I have to get up and shower too because I have to be at the hospital in a couple of hours." Leah informed me.

"So, do I. I have a kidney transplant this morning."

"I know I'm scrubbing in with you. Why don't we shower together?" Leah said and got out of the bed naked and walked into the bathroom that was connected to her bedroom, and I quickly followed behind her.

Leah turned on the shower and got into the shower and I quickly stripped out of my boxers and joined her. As we showered Leah gently massaged my body with soap and that led us to us having sex in the shower.

After we finished showering, I dried off and put back on the same clothes I had on last night. I called a cab and told Leah that I

would see her at the hospital. Before I left I gave Leah one
thousand dollars of the five thousand dollars I had won last night.
I felt I owed it to her. She introduced me to the place and she
showed me a great time last night. She gladly accepted the money.
I knew I needed to get to the bank to deposit the money because I
didn't like walking around with this much money. When the cab
arrived, the driver drove me to the lounge and I was happy to see
my Porsche was exactly where I left it. I paid the driver and
quickly unlocked the and got inside my Porsche and headed home.

On the drive home, my mind was racing. I was trying to come
up with a good lie to tell Miranda. I had never stayed out all night
and I most certainly never cheated on her. I could lie to myself
and say that I wouldn't sleep with Leah again but I knew I would.

When I pulled in the drive-way I felt a moment of relief
because I didn't see Miranda's Mercedes. I quickly got out of the
car with my bag and went into the house. I quickly went upstairs
and into my room.

"You didn't come home last night dad."

I jumped in surprise and turned around to see Kendra standing
in the doorway. "Kendra, you scared me I forgot you were
suspended from school. And I didn't come home last night and
that's between your mother and me. You just need to get your act
together." I scolded her.

Kendra just studied me for a moment and then she shook her
head and walked away. I would have talked to her further but I
needed to get ready for work. I went into the walk-in closet and
changed into jeans and a shirt. I would change into my scrubs

once I got to the hospital. I then went into the bathroom and brushed my teeth.

After brushing my teeth I picked up my hospital bag and the bag of money I won, and hurried out of the room I wanted to avoid Miranda because I didn't know what to tell her, but just as I walked out of the room Miranda was coming upstairs and she didn't look to happy to see me.

"So, you're finally arrive home, and now you're rushing to leave again?" she asked looking at the two bags in my hand."

"Look, Miranda I can't talk now because I have a kidney transplant this morning."

"Well your transplant is going to have to wait because we need to talk." Miranda said in a firm voice and I knew she wasn't taking no for an answer.

I turned around and walked back into the bedroom and I tried to think of something to tell her. Miranda walked in behind me.

"So where did you go last night?" she asked.

I turned around and faced her. "I went back to the hospital last night to see if they needed any help, and I helped with a few surgeries and I spent the night there in one of the on-call rooms."

Miranda studied my face and I could tell she was trying to see if I was telling her the truth. "You still should have called me and you should have never left the house like that. It was embarrassing and the children knew you didn't come home last night."

I sighed. "Yeah, I'm sorry about that, but I had a lot on my mind. Stanley died in surgery and it was all my fault and his wife is talking about suing me and the hospital."

Miranda put her hand over her mouth. "I'm sorry to hear that. You should have told me."

I shrugged my shoulders. "How could I when there was so much going on here."

"You're right, and I still didn't like how you sided with your sister over me. She made a lot of snide remarks to me this morning." Miranda complained.

"What do you expect when you didn't make her or Shannon feel welcomed?" I was starting to get annoyed now. I was reminded of why I stayed out in the first place.

"I know, but I'm your wife and you should side with me."

"Even when you're wrong?"

Miranda hesitated then said. "Well I wasn't exactly wrong. I have a lot of reasons to blame Shannon and not want them here."

I shook my head. "I don't have time to deal with this right now. I have to get to work." I said and left out of the bedroom before Miranda could say anything else.

I quickly left the house and drove to work. I thought I was making some progress but Miranda was still thinking of herself. I was feeling guilty about staying out all night and spending the night with Leah but not anymore.

CHAPTER 10

Miranda

Nathan was continuing to leave me speechless. I couldn't believe he just walked out on me again. And I wasn't entirely sure that he was telling the truth about his whereabouts last night. He seemed a little nervous. I needed to get out of the house and get this off my mind. I was going to start that by going to Kendra's school and getting her assignments for the week.

I went to Kendra's room to let her know that I was leaving, and then I headed to her school. After getting her assignments, I decided to head to my organization to see what was going on. When I arrived there, I parked my car and went inside the building.

I walked around the corner and went to Crystal's office. I knocked on the door and she told me to come in. I walked inside.

"Hey, what brings you by today?" Crystal greeted me with a smile. She was sitting behind the desk in a leather chair. Crystal Arnold is a beautiful white woman with long dark hair and tanned skin. She reminded you of one of the Kardashian girls. Crystal and I grew up in the same neighborhood and have been friends since kindergarten.

"I thought I would drop by and see what's going on." I answered and sat in the chair across from her.

"Things are going pretty good. We narrowed down the candidates to about ten girls that are all deserving of the scholarship."

"That's good." I said

Crystal studied me. "What's going on? It seems as if something is bothering you."

I sighed. "There is. Nathan's sister is staying with us, and Kendra got suspended from school for smoking marijuana."

"Wow, I know you and Sheila don't get along. And I'm sorry to hear about Kendra."

"Yes, me too. But it gets worst. Nathan and I had a fight last night and he didn't come home last night. He claims he was at the hospital working, but my gut tells me that he is lying."

"I don't know. It does sound suspicious, but Nathan has always been good to you. He's a lot better than Kirk." Crystal said shaking her head.

Kirk Arnold is Crystal's ex-husband and a retired baseball player. He was great in his hay day, but Crystal got tired of putting up with his constant cheating and she divorced him about eight years ago. Crystal and Kirk have thirteen-year old twin girls that they share joint custody with. "I know Nathan's been wonderful but I'm tired of him taking his sister's side on everything and I…." I paused.

"And I what?" Crystal asked curiously.

"I ran into David and he was looking good, and he wants to get together to catch up."

Crystal raised her eyebrow. "Don't tell me you are thinking about going?"

"I wasn't but now I'm thinking what's the harm."

"I can understand that, but maybe you just want to go because you're upset with Nathan." Crystal pointed out.

I considered what she was saying. "I never thought about it. Maybe you're right, but I still would like to meet with him."

"Well if you do just be careful. You two were once very much in love until you dropped him like a bad habit for Nathan." Crystal said and laughed.

"It wasn't like that." I said feeling guilty.

Crystal smacked her lips. "Please, you most certainly did, but don't feel bad. I think you made the right choice with Nathan."

"You're right." I said but I couldn't help but feel that things were very wrong between Nathan and I.

CHAPTER 11

Nathan

When I arrived at the hospital, I changed into my scrubs and went to meet with Dr. Linden so we could got talk to our patient together. I saw her standing by the nurse's station talking to one of her interns. I walked over to them.

"Are you ready to talk to Mrs. Whitehurst?" I asked her.

Dr. Linden looked up at me. "Of course, I'm ready, but I have to ask you if you are ready?"

"Yes, I'm ready. What happened yesterday I have put it behind me, and my focus is on giving Mrs. Whitehurst a new kidney." I answered her even though that wasn't entirely true. I was still thinking and bothered about what happened to Stanley but I wasn't about to tell her that.

"Good thing, I'm going to let Sarah observe the kidney transplant."

"That's good. Interns need to learn as much as they can." I said and looked at Sarah and smiled. We then walked down the hall to Mrs. Whitehurst's room. "Good morning, how are you feeling this morning?" I asked her.

Mrs. Whitehurst gave me a smile. "I feel blessed to finally be receiving a new kidney."

"That's what I like to hear." I said and Dr. Linden and I talked to Mrs. Whitehurst about the procedure and then I left and let Dr. Linden and Sarah get her prepped for surgery.

As I was washing my hands and getting ready for the surgery I was starting to feel a little panicky and I began to doubt myself. I kept having questions run through my mind like what if something goes wrong, and then I started thinking about the chaos in my home, and my night with Leah. I closed my eyes for a moment and said a prayer to clear my mind. After I said the prayer, I felt better. But I wondered if that meant anything because I prayed over Stanley yesterday and he died.

"Are you okay?" I heard Dr. Linden asked.

I opened my eyes to see Dr. Linden walking in the scrubbing area with Leah right behind her. "Yes, I'm fine and I'm tired of you asking me that. If you keep questioning me I'm going to remove you from my service." I spat out. Dr. Linden was really starting to annoy me.

"Calm down." Dr. Linden said and began washing her hands. "You seemed a little spaced out so I was just checking on you.

"You don't need to do that." I said. We continue to wash our hands in silence and after Dr. Linden finished she walked into the operating room where Mrs. Whitehurst was.

"Are you sure you're okay?" Leah asked me.

I turned and looked at her beautiful face, and just looking at her made me feel better. "As long as you're in there with me I'm going to be just fine."

Leah smiled at me. After we finished washing our hands we joined Dr. Linden in the operating room and Dr. Linden and I began to perform the surgery. Once we were about to place the kidney in her body something unexpected happened; my mind went blank. This never happened to me. I couldn't remember what to do next. And when I tried to will my mind to remember I started having flashbacks of Stanley's surgery and then the moment I pronounced him dead.

"Mills, what's wrong?" I heard Dr. Linden ask me, but her voice felt so far away, then I felt her removing the kidney out of my hand.

But I still couldn't move it was like I was stuck. I didn't know what was wrong with. I had never felt this way before.

"Okay, we're ready to close now." Dr. Linden said and that snapped me out of it. I began to help her close. "There is no need for you to help now. I've got it from here. You need to get it together because if I wasn't here to take over this surgery Mrs. Whitehurst would have been in major trouble."

"Look, I'm fine now, I just......." Then I stopped because I didn't know how to explain what just happened to me.

"Save it Mills." Dr. Linden said as she finished sewing Mrs. Whitehurst up.

I looked at her trying to think of a good comeback but I couldn't because I knew I just messed up an I left the operating room and headed to the attending's lounge and flopped down on the leather couch and put my hands in my face. "God what is happening to me. Please help me." I said out loud. I actually froze in surgery and couldn't remember what procedure came next. Was I being punished for cheating on my wife last night? I didn't understand. I continued to sit there and ask God for direction until I heard the door open and close and I felt someone gently rubbing my back. I opened my eyes and looked beside me to see Leah and I instantly felt better.

"Don't worry, I'm sure everything will be fine."

"I don't think so. I actually froze in surgery and Linden is going to use this against me I just know she is."

"Don't worry about Dr. Linden. Everyone knows your worth to the hospital."

I could find no comfort in those words because the way everyone saw it was that I was the one responsible for Stanley's Harlow's death. Leah continue to gently rub my back until the door opened and Leah quickly removed her arm from my back.

Dr. Linden appeared in the doorway and looked back and forth between Leah and me suspiciously. "The chief wants to see us in his office." Dr. Linden informed me.

I glared at her because I could only imagine what she told him. I slowly stood up and began walking towards the door with Leah right behind me.

"And you shouldn't be in here. This is the attending's lounge and you're just a nurse." Dr. Linden said to Leah.

"Leave her alone, Linden. She had my permission to be in there."

"I pretty sure she did." Dr. Linden said.

"I hope everything goes well with your talk with the chief." Leah said to me ignoring Dr. Linden.

"Thanks." I said, and Dr. Linden and I began to head towards to the chief's office.

"Leah's really supportive of you, huh?" Dr. Linden asked.

"Don't worry about that. I want to know what you told Chief Simpson."

"I told him the truth, that you zoned out in the middle of surgery." She told me.

I shook my head. I knew I would have some major explaining to do and I didn't know how I would get out of this one. We continued walking in silence, and when we arrived at his office Dr. Linden knocked and he told us to enter. Dr. Linden and I sat across from Chief Simpson.

"Mills what happened in that operating room?" Chief Simpson asked me, getting straight to the point.

"I don't know. My mind went blank for a moment." I answered honestly.

"It was more than a moment. You just stood there for about ten to fifteen minutes while I had to finish the surgery for you." Dr. Linden added.

Chief Simpson looked at me in disappointment. "Is this true, Mills?"

"Yes." I answered.

"I see. Dr. Linden you're excused. I would like to talk to Dr. Mills alone."

"Okay." Dr. Linden said and exited the office with a victorious look on her face.

"Mills, what's going on with you? First the surgery with Stanley Harlow goes wrong, and now you're freezing in surgery. What, did you forget how to operate?"

I thought for a moment trying to figure out how to answer. "My mind just went blank and it was like I was stuck." I answered honestly.

Chief Simpson studied me for a moment. "I think you're letting what happened with Stanley get to you. You know how it goes with surgeries. Sometimes things go wrong, and I know in this case it's different because it was Stanley, but you have to try to get past it. And until you do, I think you should take some time to get your head together."

"How much time?"

"Maybe a few weeks. Betty Harlow has decided to go ahead with the lawsuit and the meeting with our lawyers will be next week. And you have to be here. We have all our medical records and it wasn't your fault, so we should be good, but it will still reflect badly on us."

"Yes, I know that, and you're right I do need some time off."

"I'm glad you agree with me. You're an excellent surgeon; that's why I made you head of your own department, and I don't want you to let this setback ruin your career." Chief Simpson said.

We talked a few more minutes about Betty's Harlow lawsuit and then he told me to take the rest of day off. I exited his office and went to the attending's lounge to gather my things. My mind was heavy, and I needed time to think about everything.

CHAPTER 12

Nathan

After I had gathered my things, I left the hospital and drove out onto the highway. I didn't know what to do. I was off in the middle of the day and I had no idea of where to go or what to do. Then I thought about my mother. I hadn't been to see her in a while because my surgeries kept me so busy, so I decided I would go see her today.

I drove to the nursing home and parked my car and went inside the building. I walked over to one of the nurses. "Hey, I'm here to see my mother Diane."

"Hi, Mr. Mills. I haven't seen you in a while. Your mother isn't doing so well today."

I was overcome with a feeling of sadness because I knew that meant that she probably wouldn't know who I am today. Sometimes she remembered me and other times she thought I was my father. "It's okay, I want to see her anyway."

The nurse smiled at me. "Okay, she's right this way." The nurse said and walked me over to the room where my mother was sitting at the table playing checkers with some of the other patients.

I walked over to her and called her name.

My mother turned around. "Hey Reggie. I'm so glad you stopped by. You can't be all that busy as a policeman that you can't say hello to your wife."

I gulped hard trying to fight back the tears. "Yes, I came to see you." I played along. My mother stopped playing checkers and we went to sit in the visiting section.

"Are you here to take me to lunch?" she asked.

"No, I just wanted to stop by and see you."

"Okay, but I was hoping you would take me to lunch."

I looked at the woman who was responsible for me being successful like I was today, and it was very unfortunate that she couldn't enjoy it now. I wish I could talk to her about what was going on with me now. She probably would have some very good advice for me. I talked with my mother for about thirty minutes and then I promised her that I would see her soon before I left. I was hoping that she would remember that I was her son the next time she saw me.

After leaving the nursing home, I thought about where else I could go. I didn't want to go home because I didn't want to fight with Miranda, and to be honest I didn't want to tell her that I had all this time off now. I knew Miranda and I would continue to fight as long as Sheila was there. My sister was always welcome in my home, but I had to at least try to see if she could leave sooner so my wife could have some peace.

So, I decided I would go pay Darryl a visit to try to talk some sense into him. He needed to see about his wife and daughter. Whoever this woman was she couldn't be more important than Sheila. I felt a moment of guilt because I had cheated on my wife and now I understood how this sort of thing could happen, so I would try not to be so hard on Darryl. I pulled out my cell phone and dialed his number. Darryl answered on the third ring.

"Hello, Nathan I surprised it took you this long to call."

"Well, I've been busy, but I want to talk to you now. You have some free time?" I asked.

"Yes, I just got home but I'm going to leave in a few hours to install some kitchen cabinets at this couple's house."

"Okay, I'll be there in a few minutes." I said and ended the call.

I drove to my sister's house. She lived in a decent neighborhood in a nice three-bedroom home. Once I arrived, I parked in the drive-way behind Darryl's Nissan. I got out and knocked on the door.

Darryl answered the door. "Hey, Nathan." He greeted and stepped aside to let me in. I walked in the house and he shut the door behind me and we went into the living room to talk. We sat down on the couch.

"Darryl, I'm surprised you're not doing more to get your family back. I know you messed up, but you have to try to get her back. I mean you haven't stopped by my house to see Sheila and Shannon once."

Darryl looked at me in confusion the said. "Let me get this straight Sheila told you that I was the one that messed up."

"Yes, she said she caught you cheating in the house with a woman." I said giving him an odd look.

Darryl laughed bitterly. "I can't believe that woman. She was the one that got caught cheating. I came home early from the job and caught her getting it on with that lawyer she works for."

My mouth fell open in shock. "Please tell me that you're lying."

Darryl shook his head. "I'm afraid not. Your sister played you. She was the one that cheated so I told her she had to get out of this house. I thought she was shacked up with that lawyer. I wanted Shannon to stay with me, but she insisted that Shannon come with her."

"I can't believe she lied to me." I said feeling myself getting angry. I wanted to believe Darryl was lying to me, but I knew he wasn't. "Look I'm sorry to hear that man. Is there any way you two can work it out?"

"Not a chance. She actually told me she was in love with him."

I stood up. I didn't want to hear anymore. "I'm sorry I accused you."

"No problem. I know Shelia painted me as the bad guy, and she knew you would believe her and come to her rescue."

"I'm going to go talk to her now, and sorry again." I said and started walking towards the door.

"Wait a minute." Darryl called out to me, and I turned around

"What is it?" I asked. Darryl began to tell me a story I couldn't believe. After he finished telling me the story I was so angry I had to get out of that house immediately.

I got inside my car and drove away feeling angry. I can't believe I allowed Shelia to get one over on me like that. Miranda was right all along. I was always so protective over Shelia and my mother after my dad died, and then her rape happened, so I promised myself that I would always protect her. I felt like I was the head of the household after my father died, but Shelia wasn't who I thought she was. So now I had to get my house in order and I owed my wife a big apology. I decided to drive to the mall to pick her out a gift.

When I arrived at the mall I looked around for a minute before I started walking around. It was busy with people shopping. I felt out of place because I never had time in the middle of the day to go to the mall. After standing there for a moment looking around I walked through the mall and in a few stores. I bought Miranda a couple of expensive hand bags and then I left the mall and headed to the jewelry store. When I arrived at the jewelry store I bought Miranda a nice diamond bracelet with earrings to match.

"Your wife is going to be so happy with this." The young woman said with a smile as she rung up my purchase.

"I sure hope so." I said.

I left out of the jewelry store and got inside my Porsche and my cell phone rang. It was Leah. I answered it.

"How did it go with the chief?" she asked.

"He told me to take some time off."

"Maybe that's what you need. How about we meet up again tonight?" she suggested.

I thought for a moment. I had planned on spending the night at home apologizing to my wife and having a talk with Sheila, but I had so much fun with Leah, and being at the Lounge really made me feel alive. "Sure." I said wondering what I was going to tell my wife.

"Great, we can meet at my place like we did last time."

"Okay." I said and ended the call. I sighed. I knew I was getting myself in deep with Leah but she was a welcome distraction.

CHAPTER 13

Miranda

I was at home in the kitchen helping Shelia fix dinner. After talking to Crystal, I came to my senses. I knew that meeting up with David would be a bad idea, so I decided to go home and make the best of the situation. I was making the salad while Shelia was putting the finishing touch on the lasagna. We surprisingly didn't get into an argument. Kendra and Shannon walked into the kitchen.

"It sure smells good in here." Shannon said.

"I know. Is dinner almost ready?" Kendra asked.

"Yes, get the garlic bread out of the oven." I instructed Kendra.

Kendra went and got the garlic bread out of the oven and Kendra and Shannon set the table and I called Tim down so we could eat. I normally would have waited for Nathan but I didn't know how long he would be. I called him earlier, but he didn't answer his phone. It was something he was making a habit of. We began to eat and I heard a key turn in the door and a few moments later Nathan walked into the kitchen.

"It sure smells good in hear and I can't wait to eat some of that lasagna." Nathan said looking at our plates.

"Sorry we didn't wait for you to join us, but you didn't answer you phone earlier so I didn't know when you would be coming home." I said with a tight smile. Nathan studied my face and I know he knew I was upset.

The House Always Wins   Shanika Roach

"Sorry dear, I was in surgery most of the day." Nathan said and went to the cabinet and got a plate and then sat at the table with us and began putting lasagna on his plate.

"What surgeries did you do today?" I asked Nathan.

Nathan hesitated for a moment then said. "I had a kidney transplant and a few other surgeries that I'm sure you don't care to hear about."

"No, I want to know that's why I asked you." I said a little too sharply. Something was off about Nathan.

Everyone was quiet at the table for a moment and then Tim said. "I decided I'm going to Princeton."

"That's great." Nathan said.

I was quiet for a moment. I was happy, but I was hoping he would go to Stanford because it was closer.

"What do you think, mom?" Tim asked noticing my silence.

"That's wonderful, but to be honest I was hoping you would choose Stanford because it's closer."

"I know, but I prefer Princeton.

"You have to let him go and let him live." Sheila said, and I gave her a sharp look and to my surprise Nathan was giving her an annoyed look as well. *What is that all about?*

"That's great Tim. I will probably go to a college right here in Arizona." Shannon said.

72 | P a g e

I looked at Kendra. She was ignoring everyone and eating, and I knew she probably was jealous of the attention that Tim was getting.

"Are you going to miss me when I'm gone?" Tim asked Kendra.

"Yes, because when you leave mom and dad will probably be much harder on me."

"We're hard on you because we want you to be the best you can be and getting caught smoking in school is not your best." Nathan said firmly.

Kendra sighed. "It won't happen again, dad."

"It better not." Nathan said.

After that things were a little tense at the table, but Sheila broke the silence by talking about work and I noticed that Nathan seemed annoyed every time Sheila spoke. After dinner Nathan told the kids to leave the kitchen because he needed to talk to Sheila and me. I was confused about what he wanted to talk to us about.

After the kids left Nathan looked at Sheila. "I spoke to Darryl today."

"You did?" Sheila asked nervously.

"Yes, you care to tell me why you lied to me?"

"Okay, what's happening right now?" I asked

"Nathan, I think we should talk about this in private."

"No, we're going to talk about this in the open. My wife deserves to know what's been going on."

Sheila put her head down.

"I can't believe you would come to my house with this sob story about Darryl cheating on you when you were the one that was caught cheating." Nathan revealed.

"What, you cheated on Darryl?" I asked Shelia.

"Stay out of it. This doesn't concern you."

"Yes, it does when you bring this into my home." I said.

A humbled look came across Sheila's face and then she said. "Look I'm sorry I lied to you two, but I was embarrassed to tell you that I cheated on my husband."

"So, you make him out to be the bad guy?" Nathan asked not letting her off the hook. I was glad that Nathan was finally seeing his sister for who she truly was.

"I know it was wrong, but I'm in love with Calvin."

"Who is Calvin?" I asked.

"Calvin is the lawyer she works for." Nathan said.

I opened my mouth wide in shock. Shelia was having affair with her boss. I shook my head.

"Don't judge me. I can't help that I fell in love with Calvin, and I'm moving in with him. I'll be out of here by the weekend."

"You're moving in with him and you're not even divorced yet? How is that going to look to your daughter? That's setting a bad example don't you think?" I said in disbelief.

"Don't worry about that. I explained everything to Shannon and she understands, and I want to point out that my daughter wasn't the one who was caught smoking weed, so who looks like the bad parent right now."

I was about to say something, but Nathan cut me off. "If this is what you choose to do then that's on you Sheila, but don't put me in the middle of it, and there is something else you lied about." Nathan revealed.

I looked at Nathan in confusion and then I looked at Shelia and she had a scared look on her face.

"From the look on your face, I take it you know exactly what I am talking about." Nathan said angrily.

"He didn't tell you that did he?" Sheila asked with a tremble in her voice.

"Yes, he told me how the sex between you and Ben that day was consensual, and you only lied to save face."

"You lied about being raped, and had a man sent away for ten years!" I yelled in shock.

"Miranda, I'm warning you to shut your mouth!" Sheila screamed at me.

"Don't tell my wife to shut up. Ben was guilty of statutory rape, but the two of you had been secretly hooking up behind my mother's back for months."

Shelia began to cry, and I didn't feel one ounce of sympathy for her.

"How could you sleep with your mother's boyfriend?" I asked angrily. I didn't understand how someone could do their own mother that way.

"I didn't mean for it to happen. Ben was always extra nice to me and he offered to buy me nice things if I would do something extra for him, and since I had a crush on him anyway I took him up on his offer. I guess I just needed a father figure."

"Oh no you don't. You're not going to use Dad's death to justify this. You did it because you wanted to. You could have told mom when Ben propositioned you, but you didn't and that tells me what kind of person you really are. And then you lie on your own husband so that is just more evidence of the true you."

"No, Nathan. I'm really not a bad person." Shelia pleaded.

I was frozen in shock. I always expected there was more to Shelia's rape story, but to hear her admit it was still shocking. "Sheila I can't even look at you right now, just leave my house now." Nathan said and started walking out of the kitchen and I followed behind him and we both walked upstairs to our bedroom.

"I can't believe she lied on her husband like that, but you know I knew there was something off about her husband's alleged cheating because what woman leaves her house after she catches her man cheating. You would think she would have kicked him out, and what she just revealed I just can't wrap my mind around what she could have possibly been thinking." I said.

"I know, and I'm sorry about all this. Shelia is definitely not who I thought she was, and I don't know when I can stomach laying eyes on her again. I should have listened to you and put you first and I have something for you." Nathan said and walked to our closet. He came back with a few shopping bags and handed them to me.

I smiled at him and looked in the bags. There were two beautiful leather handbags, but when I opened the next hand bag and saw the jewelry box I hurried up and opened it, and was stunned to see a beautiful diamond earrings and necklace. "Thank you, baby." I said and hugged Nathan and gave him a passionate kiss. Then something just occurred to me. "Baby when did you have time to buy me these things?" I asked.

Nathan seemed taken aback by my question for a moment but he quickly recovered. "Oh, I had a break between one of my surgeries and I went out and bought you these things."

Something seemed off by his answer, but he did buy me these nice things, so I didn't want to ruin the moment. "I'm really going to put it on you tonight." I said seductively and reached over to kiss him again but to my surprise Nathan pulled away.

"About that baby, I need to head back to the hospital. I have a few more surgeries to do."

I frowned. "You're doing a lot of surgeries lately."

"I know baby, but one of the other general surgeons are out and I have to pick-up the slack." Nathan said and gave me a peck on the lips.

I watched as Nathan picked up his work bag and left the room. I was speechless. The good mood I was in was gone. I was feeling so great. Nathan had put his sister in her place and then he bought me these amazing gifts and then I realized that her probably bought me these gifts because he was feeling guilty. I know he was making up for putting Shelia before me but I wondered if it was more to it than that and that nagging thought wouldn't leave my mind.

CHAPTER 14

Nathan

I quickly got in my Porsche and pulled out of the drive-way hoping that Miranda bought my story. I know I was wrong for lying to my wife, but after everything that had happened in my life I needed to do something for myself. And going to this lounge and spending time with Leah was one of those things. I always put so much pressure on myself to do everything right and try to be there for my family that I felt myself breaking down. My mother didn't know me, my sister wasn't who I thought she was, and my daughter was becoming more and more rebellious. I could feel her resent towards me, Miranda, and Tim. I had a feeling that things were going to get worse with her. After that failed surgery on Stanley, I was at my whits end and then freezing in surgery the way I did I knew I needed a break. I always relied on God in my time of need like my mother taught me, but even that didn't seem to be working so this new thing I was doing was providing me with the comfort that I needed.

I called Leah on speaker phone and told her I was on my way. She was happy to hear from me and told me she was starting to get ready now. I arrived at her home ten minutes later and parked in the parking lot and I was buzzed in. I took the elevator to Leah's floor and when I arrived at her door she opened the door with a big smile on her face.

"Come on in. I'm almost ready." She said and stepped aside so I could enter her apartment.

I sat on the couch and Leah went upstairs to finish getting dressed. I felt so relaxed sitting on her couch and I was ready to head to the lounge. Leah came down about ten minutes later looking spectacular in blue jeans and a yellow blouse.

I stood up. "You look great." I complimented.

"Thank you." Leah said

We left the her condo and got inside my Porsche and I drove us to the lounge. When we went inside the lounge, I immediately felt a rush looking at everyone having a good time. Leah and I headed to the back around the corner to play poker.

When we entered Harry looked at us with a smile. He was sitting at the table with a beautiful Latina woman. "Glad to see you guys are back he said with a smile. Kate and I were about to get a game started." Harry said.

"I'm happy to back." I said and sat at the table and Leah sat next to me. Harry began dealing cards and he started the pot at one thousand dollars. I was glad I had brought the bag of money with me. As we began to play, I noticed that Harry and Kate were more than just friends, and I wondered where his wife was tonight. But what could I say, Leah and I were more than just friends. I won the next two games easily with four of a kind and a straight flush. I had won five thousand dollars at this point and I began to feel that rush again.

"You are really lucky doc, or maybe it's Leah." Harry said and winked at Leah.

I looked at Leah and she smiled at me and I wondered if she was my good luck charm. "You know what, maybe you're right." I said.

After I won another hand, Leah stood up. "That's enough poker for me, I'm going to go sit at the bar for a little while." She said.

I looked up at her and scanned over her body, and I didn't like the idea of guys checking her body out and trying to hit on her. I knew that's what would happen if she went to the bar. "No, baby why don't you sit here with me." I said surprising myself.

Leah laughed. "I've already lost over a thousand dollars."

"Yeah, I can understand that." I said. Leah left the table.

"Wait a minute, I'll join you." Kate said and quickly walked off behind Leah.

Harry chuckled. "The women can't hang with us. Leah and you are an item, huh?" he asked with a grin.

His question kind of made me uncomfortable, but then again, I was flaunting Leah out in the open.

Harry chuckled. "Don't get shy on me now Doc. It's okay I indulge myself with a few women on the side myself. It's something every man needs. Dealing with drama and the feelings of one woman is hard and we need to relieve the tension outside our relationship."

I nodded my head. He was exactly right. Leah helped me to forget about the things I was dealing with at home. Harry and I played a few more hands and, a few more people joined me and I won over fifteen-thousand dollars.

"You are on such a winning streak." Harry said shaking his head, and the other players agreed with him.

After that the other players left, and Harry and I talked for a little while longer and then I put the money I won into a bag and then headed to the bar area where Leah and Kate were sitting. Both of them were holding a drink, and just as I suspected two men were all in their faces. I walked over to the bar and put my arms around Leah.

"Oh, she's with you. I didn't know." The man said pleading his case.

Leah laughed. "We were just talking and conversing and there is nothing wrong with that."

The two-gentleman walked away and Kate said. "I'll see you guys again soon I hope. I'm going to see Harry now." She said and walked away.

"Were you jealous just now?" Leah asked and then took a sip of her drink.

"Maybe I was." I said and put my arms around her waist.

Leah put her drink down and put her arms around my neck. "Are you ready to get out of here?" she asked as she gazed into my eyes.

"Yes, I am." I answered knowing we were about to have a hot and steamy night.

CHAPTER 15

Miranda

The nerve of that man not coming home again. When I woke up and saw that Nathan wasn't beside me I immediately called him, and it was no surprise that he didn't answer. I was so upset that I was thinking about going to the hospital to talk to him, but I was afraid that things would get ugly and I didn't want to bring drama to his job. Last night I wanted to talk to him about planning a birthday party for Tim next month. He would be turning eighteen.

Instead of sitting in bed worrying about where Nathan was, I decided to go ahead and get ready for the day. After I finished showering, I dressed and went downstairs to make breakfast for Kendra and me because Tim had left already left for school. Kendra came downstairs when I was almost finished making breakfast.

"Did Dad work again all night?" Kendra asked.

"Yes." I said not turning around to look at her. I didn't want her to see how upset I was.

"Do you think he was really working?" she asked.

That made me turn around. "Of course, he was working." I said

Kendra gave me a look like she didn't believe me and I turned around and finished making breakfast. This is what I hated. Nathan was setting a bad example for his daughter.

The House Always Wins   *Shanika Roach*

After I finished making breakfast, Kendra and I sat down to eat. I asked Kendra how it was going with her school work and she said she was catching up on everything and she was studying hard. It didn't know if I believed her but I accepted her explanation for the time being.

After Kendra and I finished breakfast, Kendra put the dishes in the dishwasher and I told her that I was going to step out for a little while, and then I left the house. When I stopped at a red light I pulled out my cell phone and called David and told him I wanted to meet up with him. He was happy to hear from me and he said that he was free in an hour and we agreed to meet up at a café. When the light turned green I continued driving. I truly wasn't going to call David at first, but with the way Nathan had been behaving I thought *why not?* I was curious to know what he was up to anyway.

I killed the time by stopping at a bookstore to buy some books. It was some new releases that I had been waiting to read. After I bought the books I wanted, I headed to the café and when I arrived there I parked the car and went inside the café where David was already waiting for me. When he spotted me, he waved, and I walked over to the table and sat across from him.

"It's good to see you again, and you're looking good." He said.

"Thanks, so do you." I said, and he did. He looked good in his business suit.

The waitress came over to us. "What can I get you to drink?" she asked.

"I'll have a lemonade." I said.

"Same for me." David said.

"Where you ready to order, or do you need a minute?" the waitress asked.

I was still full, from the breakfast I ate that morning. "Nothing to eat for me." David ordered a turkey and cheese sandwich. The waitress left the table.

"So, what made you decide to meet up with me?" David asked.

I stared at him for a moment. I could say that I wanted to see him because I was mad at Nathan, but I wanted to see him anyway. "I was curious about what you have been up to."

"As I told you before I'm a real estate developer and I have been helping people with their building projects all over Arizona."

"Wow, I'm impressed." David was about to say something when the waitress came back to our table and placed our drinks and Nathan's sandwich in front of him. After she left David continued speaking.

"You're surprised that I turned out so good, right?"

"Well, yeah." I said honestly.

David laughed. "I'm glad you can admit that. I remember you telling me how lazy I was compared to Nathan."

His words made me feel bad. "You were content with just living off your parents for the rest of his life." I said trying to defend myself.

David smirked. "Look who's talking. What exactly are you doing now?"

I was speechless, and he had made his point. I was perfectly content with living off of Nathan. I did have my organization, but I was hardly ever there. But I did have two kids to raise even though they were almost grown now. "You're right, but I did finish college."

David smiled. "Yes. you did."

"So how are your kids?" I asked. I had heard from his parents that he had kids.

"They're fine. I have two boys ages ten and fourteen. I hated to move away after the divorce, but I was ready to get back to my home state."

"I can understand that. My son Tim is graduating this year, and he's going to Princeton next year, and well my daughter she's another story all together, but I'm sure she'll be just fine."

David nodded his head. "Sounds like my youngest son. He's been getting in a lot of fights in school since I left California, but I'm going to have them with me for the whole summer and hopefully that will straighten him out."

David and I finished our lunch with good conversation, and I forgot all about my troubles, and when he asked if I wanted to see his new house I agreed to go with him.

CHAPTER 16

Nathan

After waking up the next morning at Leah's, I felt refreshed. But I knew I had to go home and check in with Miranda to put her mind at ease. I was sure I could smooth things over with her. After I smoothed things over with her, I planned to go back to the lounge and gamble all day. I felt an incredible rush after winning fifteen thousand dollars, and I knew I could win much more. Leah told me that she wouldn't be joining me tonight because she had to work a double shift. I was glad I had this time off because I planned to have some serious fun.

I pulled up in the drive-way and turned off the engine and headed inside the house leaving the bag of money I won last night. The only thing I was taking in the house was my hospital bag. If I was going to lie to my wife about going to work than I had to make it believable.

I got out of the car and walked up to my house. I opened the door with my key. Once inside I sighed wondering if Miranda was going to let me have it about not answering my phone. I walked through the house heading towards the stairs when I started to hear moans coming from upstairs. My heart dropped into my stomach and I wondered if karma was coming back to bite me this quick.

I slowly walked upstairs dreading what I might discover. I didn't know how I would react if I caught Miranda with another man. The moans got louder, and I started to get angry, and I hurried up the last few steps and quickly walked to my bedroom door preparing to go off, but when I opened the door my bedroom was empty. I was confused but I quickly discovered that the moans where coming from Kendra's bedroom and I quickly ran down the hall and burst the room door open and there my daughter was having sex with some guy on top of her and at that moment I snapped and I started to have flashbacks of Shelia's alleged rape and I ran over to the bed and grabbed the guy off of my daughter ignoring her screams. I slammed him into the wall and began choking him.

"Daddy no stop it, you're going to kill him!" Kendra screamed as she grabbed my arm trying to prevent me from killing the young man.

That snapped me out of it and I sat down on the bed trying to gather myself. The young man wasted no time retrieving his clothes and running out of the room. Kendra quickly picked her clothes off the floor and ran to her bathroom. She came back into the room a moment later, dressed.

"Dad, how could you do that? You almost killed him, and he could press charges." Kendra said.

I looked at her like she had lost her mind and I stood up from the bed. "You think I'm worried about him pressing charges. He had no business having sex with my fifteen-year old daughter in my house, and how old is he and what is his name?" I asked.

Kendra hesitated for a moment like she was trying to decide on whether or not to tell me his name.

"You better tell me his name now!" I demanded.

"Okay, please just stop yelling at me. His name is Devin and he's nineteen."

I shook my head. He is too old for you, Kendra, and where did you meet him?"

"I met him at the mall."

Then I became angrier as another thought came to me. "I guess the mystery of who gave you that marijuana is now solved."

"He didn't give it to me I stole it out of his drawer." Kendra confessed.

"And you think that makes it better. I don't know what's gotten into you smoking weed and having sex in my house. You are already in enough trouble and now you want to do this." I could feel myself getting angrier and angrier and I knew I needed to leave the room. "You just stay right here. I'm going to call your mother. Where is she anyway?"

Kendra shrugged her shoulders. "She just said that she was going to step out for a little while."

I left Kendra's bedroom wondering where my wife stepped out to. I walked down stairs and into the kitchen and pulled out my cell phone to call Miranda, but she didn't answer. *That's odd* I thought. She always answered my phone calls. I called her three more times and she still didn't pick up. Something felt off to me. "Where are you, Miranda?" I said out loud.

CHAPTER 17

Miranda

I was having a wonderful time at David's house catching up with him. He had a beautiful two-story home, with four bedrooms, and it was beautifully furnished. We were sitting in his den chatting. Nathan had called me numerous times, but I ignored his calls. I was enjoying myself and I didn't want to be interrupted, and besides he couldn't be bothered to answer my calls. When my phone rung again David raised his eyebrows.

"Maybe you should answer that." He said.

I shrugged my shoulders. "I don't want to. I'll answer it later."

"Whoever is calling you must really want to talk to you, and it could be an emergency." David pointed out.

"Yeah, you're right." I said and answered the phone.

"Where are you and why have you been ignoring my calls?" Nathan asked angrily.

"You have some nerve asking me why I didn't answer your calls when you've been ignoring my calls."

"I don't have time to get into you about that. You need to get home now. There is an emergency with Kendra."

My heart started racing. "What happened now?" I asked feeling myself about to panic.

"I'll tell you when you get here." Nathan said and hung up the phone.

I immediately jumped up. "I have to go. Something is going on with my daughter." I said.

"Are you okay to drive?" David asked and looked at me with concern.

That made me feel good that he was worried about me. Something that Nathan hadn't been doing lately. It seems like the only thing Nathan was concerned about was Nathan. "Yes, I'm okay to drive." There was no way I was letting him drive me home, that would only raise more questions for Nathan.

"Okay, let me know how everything goes." David said.

"I will." I said and quickly exited his house and drove home with my stomach in knots. There was not telling what Kendra had gotten herself into now.

When I arrived home, I parked behind Nathan's truck and quickly went inside the house and shut the door behind me. "Nathan." I called out.

"I'm in the kitchen." Nathan said.

I quickly walked into the kitchen and the expression on Nathan's face scared me. "What is it?"

"I came home and caught our daughter having sex with some guy in her room." Nathan said through clenched teeth.

"What?" I asked in shock.

"You heard me, and why did you leave her home unsupervised? You know she's been a loose cannon lately."

"I know that, but she isn't a baby. I should be able to run out without having to worry about her getting in trouble."

"Well that's the reality right now. Kendra has been getting in a lot of trouble lately, and where were you anyway?"

His question caught me off guard and I was speechless for a moment, but I quickly recovered. "I went shopping and I checked in on my organization."

"Okay." Nathan said staring at me intently. "But if you went shopping, where are your bags?"

"I didn't see anything I wanted."

Nathan chuckled. "Miranda you always see something you want, but you know what I'm not going to focus on that right now because we need to go upstairs and talk to our daughter."

"Yes, let's go on up and talk to her." I agreed. I was glad that he stopped questioning me.

When we arrived upstairs, we went into Kendra's room and she was laying back on the bed with her earphones in listening to music. I walked over to her and snatched the earphones out of her ears. "You are unbelievable. You just got caught having sex in our house and you're listening to music without a care in the world?"

Kendra shrugged her shoulders.

"So you have nothing to say for yourself?" I asked not believing how nonchalant she was being.

Kendra looked at me and Nathan. "I'm sorry mom and dad. It won't happen again, but you would really like Devin if you get to know him."

"I don't think so. I don't think I can like any boy that would sneak into my house to have sex with my daughter and give her drugs." Nathan said.

Anger flashed across Kendra's face. "Everyone makes mistakes dad, and you're not perfect either. You haven't been coming home at night, and you may have mom fooled but I know you probably have another woman and I told you he didn't give it to me I took it from him without his knowledge." Kendra said boldly.

I was in shock. I had convinced myself that Shannon gave her that marijuana.

"What goes on between your mother and I is our business. You just need to get yourself together. You could learn a thing or two from Tim." Nathan said angrily.

I could see the hurt look on Kendra's face and I felt Nathan had went too far. He knows how sensitive she is about Tim. "Kendra, we expect you to do better. You are grounded for a month. Come on Nathan." I said, and he and I exited Kendra's room and went downstairs and back into the kitchen.

"You were wrong for comparing her to Tim. You know she thinks we love him more."

"Maybe I shouldn't have said that, but she still could take some pointers from Tim. I don't know what we're going to do with that girl. Do you know I almost killed that boy?"

I just shook my head imagining the scene that had unfolded when he caught Kendra in the act. "We are going to love her and be patient with her." I said.

Nathan sighed. "I'll try. Look, I just stopped home to freshen up. I'm going back to the hospital."

"More surgeries, huh?" I asked sarcastically.

"Come on Miranda, I can't deal with you hounding me right now."

"Whatever, just go and do your surgeries." I said with sarcasm still in my voice.

Nathan stared at me for a moment and then disappeared upstairs. He came back down about fifteen minutes later and kissed me on the cheek. "I'll see you later, babe." He said and left the house.

I stood in the kitchen for a few minutes just thinking about everything that had just occurred and I could feel in my spirit a big storm brewing. I just hoped we would be able to survive it.

CHAPTER 18

Nathan

I couldn't get out of that house fast enough. My daughter is really out of control, and my wife's story of her whereabouts just wasn't making sense. I really needed a break. When I was in the house, I felt a strong urge from my spirit telling me to pray, but I just couldn't. I had found a new hobby to take my mind off things and that's where I was headed now.

When I arrived at the lounge, I went inside I could already feel my mood lighten. I headed into the poker room and saw Harry sitting at the table with a man that looked a lot like him.

"Hey Doc, this is my brother George." Harry introduced.

"How are you, George?"

"I'm doing well, so you're the guy that's been winning all of the poker games." George said looking at me intently.

"Yes, that's me, and I'm back to win some more games."

I joined them at the table, and it wasn't long before a few more people joined us, and the games began. I won four straight games, causing the other players to leave and I had won twenty thousand dollars.

"Wow, you really are lucky." George said looking at me in amazement.

"Yes I am." I said as I put the money in my bag. The money felt so good in my hands.

"Tell me something if you are a brilliant surgeon why are you spending your day in here? Don't you have some surgeries you should be performing?" George questioned.

I was silent for a moment. Debating whether or not to tell them the truth. "I actually took some time off to get my head together." I said.

"What's going on?" Harry asked.

I didn't really want to get into it, so I gave them the short answer. "I'm having some problems at work and at home, but I'm counting on things to get better." I said

"I get that, and gambling helps take your mind off of it." George observed.

"Yes, and since the other players chickened out I'm going to shoot some pool." I said standing up.

George and Harry laughed as I exited the room and went to play pool. I won four games of pool and won five thousand dollars off that, and then I went to their slot machines and won there too.

After I finished, I looked at my watch and saw it was 5:00 in the afternoon. I was about to make my exit when Harry stopped me.

"I see you're on a winning streak, but just remember that your luck eventually runs out, and you can lose big as well." Harry warned.

"Not me." I said feeling myself. I was on a high and I wasn't going to let anyone bring me down.

Harry laughed. "Okay Doc, I'll see you the next time."

"Okay, you'll probably see me tomorrow." I said with a chuckle and then exited the lounge.

I went to my Porsche and got inside and drove out of the parking lot and on the highway. I had just won over twenty-five thousand dollars and it felt so good, and suddenly my problems didn't seem so big anymore, and I wondered what else I could bet on. I made a mental note to check on that. Right now, I was going to buy my wife a gift and try to smooth things over with her.

CHAPTER 19

Nathan

Over the next two weeks I spent all my time indulging in my new hobby. I spent a lot of my time at the lounge and with Leah, and I didn't come home most nights. I told Miranda I was working late at the hospital or I had to stay over because I was on call. I continued to win big at the lounge and I bought lottery tickets too. I even looked on line to see what I could bet on. I saw articles about betting on the stock market, so I removed fifty thousand dollars from our savings and placed a bet on the stock market. Miranda never checked our bank account, so I wasn't worried about her finding out. I won and doubled my money. I was on a role, and I asked Leah if she would take a trip to Las Vegas with me. I was on a winning streak and I wanted to hit the casinos in Vegas. Leah was starting to worry that I was developing a gambling addiction, but I just laughed at that. To me it was a hobby, and my gambling wasn't hurting anyone. In fact, it was helping.

Miranda and I managed to put together the birthday party for Tim, and we were both so excited. I couldn't believe my son was turning eighteen and I was so proud of him. We rented out a large building for him, and we let him invite who he wanted to within reason. Of course, Kendra complained about his birthday party being so extravagant, but we told her that we would throw her a sweet sixteen birthday party this summer. Kendra was back in school, and we hadn't had any problems out of her so far.

Things were going better for me concerning work. Chief Simpson called me and told me that he convinced Betty Harlow to drop the lawsuit. He made her understand that Stanley's artery could have burst at any moment, and it just so happen that it burst during the surgery. I was happy to hear that, and Chief Simpson said I could come back to work when I was ready, but I told him that I was going to take a few more weeks off. He was surprised to hear that because he thought I would be ready to get back to performing surgery immediately, but I wasn't ready yet. I was enjoying my time off, and I was having so much fun gambling.

Things at home were going smoothly finally, and we were on our way to church. We attended Christian Faith's Church. It was one of the largest churches in Arizona and it was pastored by Bishop Scott Langley. He was an excellent Bishop.

When we arrived at church, the usher's seated us and we stood up as the choir sang. The song was soothing but mind started to wonder. I started thinking about the next thing I could place a bet on.

The music stopped ten minutes later, and Bishop Langley came to the podium. Bishop Langley was a tall brown-skinned man with a solid build in his early forties. "Good morning, everyone." Bishop Langley greeted.

"Good morning." The congregation said in unison.

"Today I want to preach about addiction." Bishop Langley started. "I actually planned to preach about something else, but last night God put it on my heart to preach about addiction, so I know this is an important message for someone."

I gulped hard wondering if this message was for me. *But I don't have an addiction, do I?* I silently asked myself.

"There are a lot of people out there that are struggling with addictions, but they don't want to admit they need help, or they are too embarrassed to talk about it. But there is no need to feel ashamed because God is here for you and I'm going to provide scriptures that can help with that. 1:Psalm 27:4-6 reads One thing I ask from the Lord, this I do seek: that I may dwell in the house of the Lord all the days of my life, to gaze on the beauty of the Lord and to seek him in his temple. For in the days of trouble he will keep me safe in his dwelling; he will hide me in his shelter of his sacred tent and set me high upon a rock. Then my head will be exalted above the enemies who surround me; at his sacrifice with shouts of joy; I will sing and make music to the Lord. The importance of this is to remind you the importance of having a real relationship with God, and when you do He will make it possible to overcome impossible situations. I know you probably feel that you can't stop craving your addiction, but nothing is too impossible for God. Next is John 16:33, and it reads I have told you these things, so that in me you may have peace. In this world you will have trouble. But take heart! I have overcome the world. This verse is a reminder that you will have to find courage and strength within yourself to beat the addiction. Obstacles will occur, but nothing is too hard for God. 1 Peter 3:11 reads They must turn from evil and do good; they must seek peace and pursue it. This means that to beat the addiction you are going to have to constantly face the demons that can trigger your addiction. To become a more happy and healthy person, it is essential to seek things that bring you joy and peace. Moreover, James 4:10 reads humble yourselves before the Lord, and he will lift you up. This means that it is important for you to realize that you don't have control over everything. There are going to be a lot of things that happen that are out of your control, and instead of dealing with these things by relying on your addiction, you should acknowledge that you are powerless and to Let God take care of you. When you do this, it will strengthen your faith. Lastly, Corinthians 4:5 reads Therefore nothing before the appointed time; wait until the Lord comes. He will bring to light what is hidden in darkness and will expose the motives of the heart. At that time each will receive their praise from God. This means that on your journey to become a more healthy and evolved person that you should eliminate judging yourself and others. While recovering there is no room for judgement. Those who keep an open mind about themselves and others are much more likely to have a closer relationship with God and enjoy all the help and love a relationship with God will bring. With God on your side you can beat your addiction."

After the Bishop finished reading all those scriptures my head was spinning and I started to feel a little claustrophobic, and I know it was only because I was trying to fight what God was trying to tell me.

"I know that was a lot of scriptures, but I can feel it's someone in this room that really needs to hear that. Whoever is struggling with an addiction, I want you to be brave enough to come to the alter now, so I can pray over you."

I looked around and a few people walked to the front, and I could feel my spirit urging me to go to the alter, but I just couldn't. I was just having fun. It wasn't as serious as the Bishop was making it out to be, I told myself, but I know it was starting to grow into something much more, but I couldn't go up there. What would Miranda and my children think?

"Last call, is there anyone else that needs to come to the alter?" the Bishop asked as he stared out into the congregation."

I sat there stubbornly refusing to move. I didn't have a problem and I refused to believe that I did. When no one else came to the alter, the bishop prayed over the few people that came to the alter. He said one last prayer before he concluded the service.

"Wow, that was powerful." Miranda said as we all stood up.

But I ignored her. I hurried out of the church. I had to get out of that building as fast as I could.

CHAPTER 20

Miranda

It was two weeks later, and the day of Tim's birthday party. We were all so excited. My handsome son was turning eighteen. We rented out a big building for him, and he invited some of his friends from school. I invited my parents, but they couldn't make it. They actually had plans to go out of town for the weekend.

Even though I was excited about Tim's birthday party, I could tell something was off with Nathan. He freaked me and the kids out when he ran out of church two weeks ago. When I questioned him about it, he said he wasn't feeling well. I didn't know if I believed it but I was going to let it go for now because things were finally going better for our family.

Nathan and I were on the way to the building we had rented out. Kendra and Tim were already there.

"I'm still not one hundred percent sold on Kendra's boyfriend." Nathan said.

"Come on we already talked about this and we agreed that we would let Kendra date him." Kendra had been begging us to give Devin a chance, but we were reluctant. Getting caught having sex with our daughter in our house isn't the best first impression, but finally Kendra wore us down and we invited Devin over. He is nineteen years old and he goes to the local community college and he says he plans to transfer to a four-year university in a couple of years. Him having plans for his future was a plus sign for us. We agreed to let Kendra date him, as long there was not a repeat of what happened the last time, and when Nathan I confronted him about the marijuana Kendra was caught with, he explained that he tried marijuana a few times, but he didn't smoke it anymore and he didn't know he still had some left over in his drawer.

"I know, but I don't know if I will ever totally like him." Nathan said.

I laughed. I couldn't blame him about that. When we arrived at the building we went inside, and the place was already filled with teenagers dancing and sitting down in chairs mingling. I spotted Tim and his girlfriend Brandy standing in the corner, and I headed in the direction with Nathan following behind me.

"Hey there you two." I greeted them and gave my son a hug. He looked handsome in his black jeans and designer shirt.

"Hello, Mr. and Mrs. Mills." Brandy greeted us. Brandy is a pretty slender light skin girl with long hair. I liked her a lot. She was smart just like Tim and she planned to go to college at Princeton as well and I wondered if that was a major deciding factor in Tim's decision.

"Hey you two should be out there dancing instead of hiding in the corner." Nathan said with a smile.

"Leave them alone Nathan. I'm sure they will dance soon."

Nathan shrugged his shoulders.

"Thanks for throwing this party for me. It really means a lot to me." Tim said.

Nathan patted Tim on the shoulder and said. "Anything for you man."

"Where is your sister?" I asked.

"She went to fix herself a plate along with Devin, Shannon, and her date." Tim told us.

"Okay, I'm going to see what she's up to." I said and began to walk away.

Nathan followed behind me. "I hope Kendra decides to behave herself at this party." Nathan said.

"I'm sure she will. She hasn't done anything lately to make us think that she won't." I said. I really wished Nathan would lighten up on Kendra. We walked around the corner and down the hall where a dining area was set up and we saw Kendra, Devin, Shannon, and her date sitting at the table. They didn't see us at first because they were so engrossed in their conversation, but Kendra finally saw us.

"Hey." Kendra greeted us with a smile.

"Hey, you guys." I said and Nathan said hi as well.

"This is a great party." Shannon said.

"I'm glad you're enjoying yourself." Nathan said and then his face turned serious.

I knew he was thinking about his sister. I told him he should invite Sheila, but he said he wasn't ready to see her yet.

"Kendra, I don't want you trying to sneak out of this party." Nathan warned.

Kendra rolled her eyes. "I'm not going to sneak out of the party."

"Okay, I'm just letting you no you better not." Nathan said and walked away from the table totally missing the hurt look come across Kendra's face.

"I don't get it. I have been on my best behavior at home and at school, and it's still not good enough for dad. He just had to embarrass me." Kendra said with a miserable look on her face.

"It's okay, your dad is just looking out for you." Devin said and that made me smile because despite what he had done, I still believed he cared for my daughter.

"Everything is going to be fine. You guys enjoy yourselves." I said and walked away from the table.

I looked around for Nathan and I didn't see him, so I fixed myself a plate and watched the teenagers enjoy themselves and as I watched them I thought about when Nathan and I had been young and in love. We were still very much in love, but I noticed a difference in his behavior. It was like he was there but not really there. He was always distracted all the time when he was home, but the majority of his time was spent at the hospital. I know he's a surgeon and surgeons have demanding careers but not that demanding.

After I finished my food, I still hadn't seen Nathan and I realized that he must have left the party, but why would he leave his son's party and without telling me? I decided to do what I have been doing for a while to take my mind off Nathan's sketchy behavior I called David. Talking to him was like a breath of fresh air and we even met for lunch over the past few weeks. David answered on the third ring.

"Hey Miranda. I'm surprised you're calling. Isn't today your son's birthday party?" he asked.

For a moment I felt foolish for calling him while at my son's birthday party, but I quickly shook the feeling off. No need to feel foolish now, he was already on the phone. "I know, but I just wanted to call you and say hi and to see how you're doing."

David laughed. "I'm doing fine, and I'm doing even better now that you've called me."

A big smile appeared on my face. He had managed to lift my mood with those few words. We began to chat, and I was so engrossed in the conversation that I didn't notice Nathan walking up until he was standing right in front of me.

"Who has you smiling like that?" Nathan asked curiously.

I froze for a moment not knowing what to do until my brain finally started working again. "I have to go." I told David and ended the call.

Nathan sat beside me. "Who was that, Miranda?" he asked squinting his eyes at me.

"That was Crystal." I said thinking quickly.

"Okay, I'm surprised she didn't come."

"Her daughter is sick." I said and then I remembered I had questions of my own that I needed answers to. "Where did you go?"

Nathan looked taken aback for a moment and then he said. "I got a page from the hospital and I went there to help one of the residents through a surgery." Nathan answered.

I stared at him searching his face for the truth. He seemed to be telling the truth, but something was telling me he was lying, but I didn't want to ruin my son's birthday party by arguing with Nathan. It was time for Tim's birthday surprise anyway and I couldn't wait to see the look on his face when he saw the new car Nathan bought him and no one deserved it more than him.

CHAPTER 21

Miranda

It was a month later and things were going well. Nathan's behavior was still off and I wondered if it was another woman. I had never worried about Nathan being with another woman before because he always told me and made me feel like I was the most beautiful woman in the world, but now I wondered if someone else had caught his eye. He didn't give me that extra special attention that he use to give me. But maybe it was something more. When I did the laundry, I found a couple of lottery tickets in his pocket, but he told me that he just had an urge to play the lottery. That was strange because Nathan had never cared about things like that before. He always said if you worked hard in life then you didn't have to rely on things like playing the lottery, and then two days later he came home happy because he said he won three hundred dollars off of the lottery ticket. His face had this unbelievable look of joy on it that I had never seen before. Even though something didn't feel right, I just took his word for it because I know that whatever was done in the dark would come to light anyway and I needed to keep that in mind for myself since I was having secret meetings with David. I tried to convince myself that they were harmless, but the stranger Nathan's behavior becomes the more I find myself growing closer to David. The closer I got to David the more I started to think what if?

Other than that, I couldn't complain too much, and Tim was enjoying his new car and Kendra seemed happy for her brother, but I could see the jealousy in her eyes, and I told her maybe she would get a car for her sixteenth birthday this summer if she continues on the right path.

I was just about to leave the house to pick up some things for dinner when the house phone rang. I started to ignore it and just leave the house, but something told me not to, so I turned around and hurried to answer the phone in the living room before it stopped ringing. I answered the phone.

"Hello is this Mrs. Mills?"

"Yes, may I ask whose calling?"

"I'm Deborah Stein the nurse at Gaston Academy. Kendra is throwing up constantly. I took her temperature and it's normal. It could be something she ate, but I would advise you to take her to the hospital just to make sure it's nothing serious."

"Okay, I will be there as soon as I can." I said and quickly left the house. I drove quickly to the school wondering what was going on with Kendra because she seemed fine when she left the house this morning.

When I arrived at the school, I quickly parked and went into the building. One of the teachers in the hallway showed me where the nurse's office was. When I went into the office, Kendra was sitting in the chair and she wasn't looking too good. I quickly walked over to her. "Kendra, you don't look so good."

"I don't feel so good either." Kendra said weakly.

The nurse walked around the corner. "Hello, you must be Mrs. Mills. Kendra maybe has a stomach virus or something." The nurse said.

After talking with her for a few more minutes Kendra and I left the school and I headed to the doctor's office.

"Mom, I really don't want to go to the doctor. I'll be fine really."

"Maybe so, but I don't want to take any chances." I said.

When we arrived at the office, we went inside, and Kendra signed in and we waited to be called. Twenty minutes later the nurse called us back. The nurse took us to the exam room, and we waited for the doctor.

The doctor came in a few minutes later and introduced herself. After asking Kendra a few questions she took Kendra to get a blood and urine sample, and Kendra came back to the room about fifteen minutes later with a nervous look on her face.

"What's wrong, honey?" I asked her.

"I'm just scared that something is really wrong with me."

"Oh, don't worry about that taking blood and urine samples is routine when the doctors are trying to find what's wrong with you." I tried to reassure her.

We waited patiently until the doctor finally came back to the room about an hour later with a very serious expression on her face.

"What is it?" I asked her, feeling myself about to panic.

The doctor hesitated and looked back and forth between me and Kendra.

"Is it that bad?" Kendra asked in a broken voice.

"No, calm down. You aren't dying or anything, but you are pregnant?" The doctor revealed.

Something inside me snapped and I could feel the rage churning in my stomach. "How can you be pregnant? Do you have any idea what this will do to your future, not to mention how your father will react!" I yelled. I didn't care if we were in the doctor's office. I couldn't believe she had gotten herself into this type of situation.

Kendra started crying and the doctor sat down in the chair across from us.

"Listen, I know this is a lot to take in and Kendra you're only fifteen, but you guys can get through this. If you decide that you can't deal with this there is always other options."

Anger flashed across Kendra's face. "I'm not killing my baby." Kendra said her voice trembling.

"There is always adoption if you don't want to have an abortion." The doctor continued.

Kendra was about to say something else, but I interrupted her. "Listen, we don't know what we are going to do, but how far along is she?"

The doctor said she needed to examine Kendra further, so she could see how far along she is, and I left the room so she could examine her. After the examination, she told me that Kendra was six weeks pregnant. She told Kendra she wanted to see her back in four weeks and gave her some prenatal vitamins and we left the doctor's office.

On the drive home, my mind was all over the place. Everything was going better, and this is the last thing that our family needed. I cringed when I thought about how Nathan would react.

"Mom please don't make me have an abortion. We're Christians and Christians aren't supposed to have abortions." Kendra pleaded with me.

"Don't try to give me a lesson about what Christians shouldn't do because Christian's aren't supposed to have premarital sex either and I'm assuming Devin is the father?" I asked her.

"Of course, mom, I don't sleep around."

When we arrived home, Kendra rushed upstairs to her bedroom and shut the door. I went in the kitchen and sat down at the table. I didn't know what to do. My daughter being pregnant at fifteen felt like a nightmare. I know taking Kendra to have an abortion went against everything I believed in, but that was what I was strongly considering. I could take her to have an abortion and Nathan wouldn't have to know anything about it. Every since he caught Kendra and Devin in her room he had been extremely hard on her and he had every reason to be but still he needed to lighten up on her a little. I sat at the table for about twenty minutes trying to decide what to do. I knew I should pray about it, but I knew what God wanted me to do. As I sat there thinking I finally made a decision about what I was going to do.

CHAPTER 22

Miranda

I woke up early the next morning and went downstairs to make breakfast for my family. I didn't have an appetite, but I was going to force some food down anyway.

"Look at you up super early making breakfast." Nathan said and kissed me on the cheek.

"Yes, I just felt like getting up early." I said as I flipped the pancakes over and glanced over at Nathan as he got glasses out of the cabinet.

Nathan actually came home early last night, and I wasn't happy about that at all. I was hoping that he would stay late at work or not come home at all because I had a hard time convincing Kendra that getting an abortion is what she needed to do. She was upset because she wanted to talk to Devin about it, but I told her that the last thing he probably wanted was a baby. Kendra looked hurt, but she finally came around to the idea. I had to console her for about an hour as she cried. I told Nathan that Kendra wasn't going to school today because she was sick. When Nathan came home he noticed that something was bothering me. I told him I was alright. Nathan was all over me last night wanting sex, which is something that he hasn't been wanting much from me in a while. I had been missing that, but last night I was not in the mood and I told Nathan so. He was surprised but he didn't press me about it.

Tim came downstairs about twenty minutes later and we ate breakfast. I was quiet, but Nathan was in a good mood and he talked about a surgery that he would be performing today. After we finished breakfast, Nathan and Tim left and I went upstairs to Kendra's bedroom and she was still laying under the covers but she wasn't sleep.

"Kendra get out of that bed, you know we have an appointment this morning." I ordered her. They had to squeeze her in as it was, so I definitely didn't want to be late.

Kendra slowly sat up in bed with a pitiful look on her face. "Mom please don't make do this."

I blew out a frustrated sigh. "Kendra, we have been over this and we are doing this so get up and get ready now. I'm going to go downstairs, and you better come downstairs within the next twenty minutes or I'm going to drag you out of this house." I demanded and left out of her room and slammed the door and went downstairs. I know I was extra hard on her, but I was already on edge. This was not an easy decision to make, so it was best if we just went ahead and do it as planned with no delays. I had called a clinic in Florence because I didn't want to take a chance of running into anyone I knew in Phoenix, so we had about a little over an hour drive.

Finally, Kendra came downstairs and we left the house and I drove to Florence. The car ride was quiet, and I was glad. It gave me a chance to clear my mind. When we arrived at the clinic we went inside and signed in and took a seat.

As we waited my stomach was in knots and I knew I was making the wrong decision but having to deal with Kendra being pregnant seemed like too much for the family to handle. Finally,

Kendra was called to the back and I prayed to God that this decision wouldn't come back to haunt me.

CHAPTER 23

Nathan

Two weeks had passed by and everything was going well at work. I thought jumping back into surgery would be hard, but it wasn't. I was back to myself again as far as work goes. But I had to admit that my new hobby had a lot to do with it. I left Tim's birthday party because I got a call about placing a bet on the stock market. I removed two hundred thousand dollars from my bank account to bet on the stock market and I won and doubled the money. I continued to win big and the lounge too.

I was still seeing Leah and things had been growing pretty well with her, but Miranda was a whole different story. Miranda really was on edge lately and Kendra seemed depressed and I noticed she and Miranda weren't really speaking. When I asked Miranda about it she dismissed it saying you know how teenagers are. I felt like there was something more, but I was going to leave it alone for now.

I was getting ready to repair a damaged kidney, I was half way through the surgery when Dr. Linden came into my operating room. Since I had been back Dr. Linden had been staying out of my way as much as she could. I guess she felt a little guilty for throwing me under the bus, so I was surprise to see her.

"Dr. Mills I'll take over for you because you have a family emergency." She told me.

I stopped what I was doing. "What happened?" I asked in shock.

"Your daughter was brought in."

"What happened to her." I asked as my heart started racing.

Dr. Linden looked at the floor before looking back up at me and I knew it was bad because I had never really seen Dr. Linden nervous like this before.

"I don't have all the details, but I do know she was rushed into surgery and Dr. Gilbert is performing her surgery."

Dr. Gilbert was a gynecologist. *Why did Kendra need a surgery by a gynecologist?* I wondered, but I knew I had no time to waste. I stepped away from the table and removed my surgical gloves and quickly left the operating room and headed to the gynecology department.

When I arrived there, I saw my wife sitting in the waiting room with a dreadful look on her face. I quickly went over to her. "Miranda what happened?"

Miranda looked up at me and started trembling. I sat beside her and wrapped my arms around her to stop her trembling. "Try to calm down and tell me what happened."

Miranda looked into my eyes and I saw that her eyes were filled with remorse. "I took Kendra to have an abortion a couple of weeks ago and she developed an infection." Kendra revealed.

And there it was the reason for her and Kendra's strange behavior. I had no idea it was something like this and I could feel anger swelling up inside me. "You took our daughter to have an abortion without talking to me?" I asked through clenched teeth.

Tears started spilling down Miranda's cheeks. "I'm sorry, I found out she was pregnant a couple of weeks ago, and I thought having an abortion was the best option for her."

"Clearly it wasn't because you took her to a doctor that botched her surgery. This family doesn't believe in abortion and you know that, now look what happened."

I was about to continue my tirade when I was interrupted by Dr. Gilbert. She had a somber look on her face and I knew it was bad. "How bad is it?" I asked.

"The infection to Kendra's uterus is pretty severe and our only option is to perform a hysterectomy, or the infection could further spread and kill her." Dr. Gilbert informed us.

I felt my heart breaking into a million pieces and Miranda began to cry uncontrollably. I hated that my daughter wouldn't be able to have children, but it was either that or she would die.

"Okay, do what needs to be done." I said.

"Okay, and I will send one of the residents out to keep you updated." Dr. Gilbert said and walked away.

"How could you tell her to go ahead and do the surgery. Kendra's only fifteen and she will never be able to be a mother. I had to force her to get an abortion. She will never speak to me again." She said between sobs.

I looked at my wife and it broke my heart to see her falling apart this way, but this was all her fault and I wasn't going to provide her with any comfort. "You should have thought about this before you took our daughter to have an abortion. You should be ashamed of yourself." I said.

Miranda continued to cry and I ignored her and stared off into space wondering how my daughter would cope with all this. An hour later a resident came out to tell us that Kendra was stable. We waited a few more hours and finally later Dr. Gilbert came around the corner and walked over to us.

"The hysterectomy was a success. Kendra is stable, and she is in recovery. You can see her after we get her settled in, and I'm terribly sorry about all this." Dr. Gilbert said sincerely.

"Thank you for saving my daughter's life." I said.

Dr. Gilbert nodded and walked off, and a nurse came to get us about twenty minutes later and we went in to see Kendra. She was still unconscious and just looking at her made me want to fall apart but I had to keep it together. Miranda and I each took a seat on the side of her bed. Miranda held Kendra's hand until finally she opened her eyes.

Kendra looked around in confusion and then her eyes rested on us. "What happened to me?" she asked.

"Remember I had to call an ambulance for you because you were in severe pain." Miranda said. Kendra slowly nodded her head. Miranda tried to continue but she started crying and I knew I had to step in. As a doctor I knew that delivering bad news was never easy, and you just had to come right out and say it, but it was different because this was my daughter.

I hesitated a moment before speaking and then I said. "You developed an infection because of the abortion you had, and you had to have a hysterectomy." I informed her.

Kendra frowned. "What exactly does that mean for me?" Kendra asked.

I felt a knot forming in my throat. "It means that you won't be able to have any children." I choked out.

"What?" Kendra said in shock and then she looked at Miranda and anger flashed across her face. "This is all you fault. You made me do this, and I hate you!" Kendra shouted, and tears started to stream down her face.

"I'm so sorry." Miranda said.

I couldn't take it anymore and I got up and left out of the room and went into the attending's lounge. I felt like punching a whole through the wall.

Leah came into the lounge. "I heard about your daughter. How did everything go?" Leah asked.

"Not now, Leah." I snapped.

A hurt look flashed across Leah's face, but she nodded in understanding and left.

I didn't mean to snap at her I just really needed to be alone right now. I was trying to make sense of what was happening to my family. As angry as I was with Miranda, I knew I had some blame in this too. I had been neglecting my family and being selfish. I felt this overwhelming feeling to pray, but I ignored it. I was going to do the one thing that took my mind off everything, but this time I was going to do it big. I was going to plan a trip to Las Vegas to hit the casino, and I was going to take Leah with me, and I started to feel better just thinking about it.

CHAPTER 24

Miranda

It was two weeks after Kendra's surgery, and she still had about four to six more weeks before she fully recovered. Her body was different now, and the doctor explained to her all of the different changes her body will have now one being that she would no longer have a menstrual cycle. And that was a lot for a girl her age to take in. Kendra was deeply depressed and I apologized to her profusely, but she still hated me and she barely talked to me. When she told Devin what happened he was upset that Kendra didn't tell him she was pregnant, but he still came by to check on her. Tim couldn't believe what happened and even he looked at me differently.

I felt like crap and Nathan was upset with me as well and he only stayed home a few nights in the past few weeks. He gave his usual excuse of having extra surgeries but I knew he just didn't want to be around me and I couldn't really blame him. I had made a decision that scarred my daughter's life and would affect her future. I prayed to God to give me strength and that helped some. I had barely had any sleep over the last two weeks.

It was Saturday afternoon and Tim was out playing basketball with a few of his friends and Kendra was in her room listening to music. Nathan had left last night for a doctor's convention. I needed to get out of the house to get some fresh air so I went upstairs and told Kendra I was leaving. She just nodded her head without looking at me. I left her room wondering if me and my daughter's relationship would ever be the same.

I grabbed my purse and keys and left the house. I was going to go and visit Crystal for a little while. I really needed a shoulder to lean on. David had been calling me wanting to meet up for lunch, but I told him I couldn't. My focus needed to be on my family right now.

I drove to Crystal's house. She lived in a nice three-bedroom condo. I parked my car and went to her door and knocked.

Crystal opened the door a moment later. "Hey Miranda, what a nice surprise." She said with a smile and stepped aside to let me in. She shut the door behind me and we went into her living room and sat down on her green sectional sofa.

"I'm sorry to drop by like this, but I really needed to get out of the house." I said.

"No problem at all. You know you're welcome here anytime. The girls are with Kirk this weekend, so we have plenty of privacy to talk."

I shook my head. "Crystal, I have made such a mess of my life. I don't think Kendra and I's relationship will ever be the same." I said sadly.

Crystal gave me a sympathetic look. "Time heals all wounds and I really believe your relationship with her will eventually get better."

"I wish I could believe that, but it just seems so hard."

"I know, but you really shouldn't have taken her to get that abortion." Crystal said.

"You're right I shouldn't have but I just didn't want to deal with my daughter having a baby and Nathan would have exploded. I thought it would be better for everyone if she had the procedure."

Crystal studied me for a moment and then said. "Now you see it would have been better to just deal with your daughter having a baby at sixteen, and if she felt like she couldn't raise it adoption would have been an option."

"I wish I would have really took the time to really think about all this, but I made a rush decision." I said.

"Yes, you did, but what's done is done and now you have to just deal with the aftermath. It may take a while, but I really feel like your family will return back to normal."

I gave Crystal a half smile and I could feel myself starting to feel better. Crystal always gave me good advice and told me the truth without being harsh. I spent the remainder of the afternoon talking with Crystal and we even ordered a pizza and watched a movie, and for just that moment my life felt good.

CHAPTER 25

Nathan

Leah and I had an amazing time in Vegas Friday night. We had an amazing dinner and we checked out some of the popular places and we went shopping as well, but today we were hitting the casino and I had withdrawn three hundred thousand dollars from my bank account to gamble with.

I was headed to the craps table with Leah by my side. We were both looking sharp in our new clothes. I called for eight and when the dice rolled it was six and I lost, but that didn't shake me. But then I kept losing and losing, and Leah whispered in my ear that maybe I should stop but I didn't listen to her and I eventually lost all the money and that was a new feeling for me because I was so use to winning.

I left the table and headed over to the ATM machine to get some more money out and Leah was right behind me. When I arrived at the machine I was about to put my card in when Leah grabbed my hand.

"Nathan you need to stop. You just lost all your money, so you need to quit while you are ahead." She warned me.

"No, I don't. I need to keep playing until I win my money back or at least double it."

Leah shook her head. "Nathan you have a problem. You need to get some help."

"I don't have a problem I can stop anytime I want, and I'm not hurting anyone."

"And those are a couple of things that an addict says." Leah informed me.

When she called me an addict I immediately started to think back the Bishop's sermon. I didn't want to be reminded of that right now, so I moved Leah's hand out of the way and extracted fifty thousand dollars from my account and then I turned to look at Leah after I got my money out of the machine. "Leah if you thought I had such a problem, why did you take this trip with me, and why have you been happily spending the money I've been winning?" I asked her sarcastically.

Leah looked hurt by my words then she said. "You know what I was just trying to warn you, but go ahead and do whatever you want to do. I'm going back to our hotel room." She said and walked away.

I shrugged my shoulders and headed back over to the craps table and it didn't take long for me to lose all my money and a sick feeling came over me and I thought *how an I going to replace the money?* Then I got an idea. Against my better judgement I went over to the ATM machine and I extracted ten thousand dollars from my bank account. I headed to the blackjack table. Blackjack wasn't really my game, but I was desperate. The dealer dealt me two cards that came to sixteen. I shook my head in frustration at the cards. I hated getting a total of sixteen in blackjack because you were pretty much stuck. But I told the dealer to hit me with another card anyway hoping I would get five, but I got a seven and busted. And from then on I lost until the ten thousand dollars was gone and I banged my hand on the blackjack table in frustration and the other players and the dealer looked at me in shock, but I didn't care that was over half of the money in my bank account gone.

"What are you guys looking at?" I yelled and the dealer looked like he wanted to alert security, so I quickly left the casino. I went to the room we had rented in the casino. When I went inside of the room, Leah was sitting in the living room area watching TV. She turned her attention to me and studied my face.

"You lost the money, didn't you?" she asked

I just nodded my head and went and sat beside her on the couch. "I can't believe I lost. I have no idea how I'm going to replace the money." Then I thought about Harry warning me about losing big. He was right. I was on such a high that I didn't think of the down side of gambling.

"I'm not sure how you're going to going to replace the money, but I'm sure you'll think of something."

"I sure hope you're right." I said and laid my head on her shoulder feeling miserable.

CHAPTER 26

Nathan

Leah and I flew back to Phoenix on Monday morning and I had finally figured out how I was going to replace the money in our bank account. Leah left her car at the airport, so she drove us back to her place where my Porsche was. When we arrived at her house I got out her car with my luggage and quickly went to my car.

Leah quickly followed me and stopped me before I could get into my car. "Are you sure you want to do this?" Leah asked me with a worried look on her face.

"Of course, I don't want to do this, but I don't have much of a choice."

Leah nodded her head in understanding and walked away from my car. I quickly unlocked my car and placed my luggage inside and then got into my car and drove away. I was headed to the bank. I was nervous as I walked into the bank. I couldn't believe what I was about to do.

When I arrived at the bank, I walked inside and waited in line for one of the tellers. Once I arrived at the front of the line, I told the teller I needed to transfer the money I set aside for my son's tuition to my bank account. She told the manager and I went back to talk to him. He was surprised and asked me if I was sure I wanted to do this, and I told him I was. Once the transfer was made I left the bank and headed home feeling like a low life.

When I arrived home, I was surprised to see that Miranda wasn't home, but I had to admit I was glad because I wasn't ready to face her yet. I went into Kendra's room to check on her.

"Hey, how are you feeling?" I asked.

Kendra looked up from the magazine she was reading and said. "I'm okay."

"Do you know where you mother is?"

"She said she had to run out."

"Okay." I said and left the room and went to my bedroom. I put my luggage in the closet then I laid on the bed.

I stared at the ceiling trying to figure out how I was going to replace my son's college tuition. I can't believe I had gotten myself into this situation. I kept telling myself that gambling was just a hobby for me and that I could stop at any time, but now I could see that I had a problem. I stared at the ceiling for twenty minutes until an idea finally came to me.

I got off the bed and went over to the dresser and went into the bottom drawer and pulled out the folder that contained all the information to Miranda's organization. Miranda had two hundred thousand dollars that she was giving away to a young lady to go to college. I had all the banking information and I could wire that money over to Tim's college fund without leaving the trace. It wasn't enough to replace his whole tuition, but it was a start and I could figure out how to get the rest of the money for Tim's tuition and Miranda's organization. I know this was a horrible thing to do, but I was desperate. Without thinking twice about it, I took the banking information and used Miranda's laptop to make the transfer. Once the transfer was made, I breathed a sigh of relief.

Now I had to make this up to Miranda somehow, and I had the perfect idea. I was going to start by making dinner. Before I did that, I went to Kendra's room to chat with her. She was slowly coming out of her depression, but she wasn't totally herself yet.

After chatting with her for a little while, I called the hospital and let them know I would be coming in tomorrow. I spend another hour looking at the news and then it was time for me to make dinner. My mom had taught me how to cook. With her working two jobs she needed plenty of help around the house. I looked in the freezer and pulled out a pack of pork chops and got some ranch seasoning out of the cabinet. I was going to bake ranch pork chops. I fixed a macaroni casserole and baked some rolls to go along with it. I even made a pitcher of lemonade.

"Dad, you're cooking?" Tim asked as he walked into the kitchen with his book bag.

"Yes, I'm cooking and don't look so surprised."

Tim laughed. "It smells good, and I can't wait to eat some."

"Good, go get your sister and tell her dinner's ready." I ordered him.

"Sure thing." Tim said and walked out of the kitchen.

I began fixing their plates and Miranda walked into the kitchen with a surprised look on her face. "You made dinner?" Miranda asked.

I chuckled. "Why is everyone so surprised. Yes, I made dinner. I wanted to surprise you. Where have you been all day?" I asked her.

"I spent some time with Crystal and I'm surprised that you been here long enough to notice I've been gone most of the day."

"Well yes, I've been here most of the day."

Miranda went upstairs and came down about five minutes later along with Tim and Kendra, and we ate dinner and had a nice conversation. Kendra didn't say much to her mother, but other than that the dinner went nice, and I was happy to spend this time with my family. Looking around at there faces at the table really let me know that I needed to figure out how to replace all the money quick.

After dinner, Miranda and I showered together and watched a movie and I made love to her like she was the last woman on earth with so much intensity. With each stroke I was apologizing to her and letting her know that I was going to do whatever I had to do get my family out this predicament I had gotten them in.

CHAPTER 27

Miranda

I woke up the next morning sore, but in a good mood. I don't know what had gotten into Nathan last night, but I liked it. He hadn't made love to me like that in a long time. I got up and took a shower and then went downstairs. Tim was finishing up a bowl of cereal.

"I would have made you some breakfast." I told him.

"That's okay mom, I was in the mood for some Frosted Flakes this morning."

I laughed and went to make Kendra and I some breakfast. After Tim finished eating his cereal he kissed me on the cheek and left for school. After I finished making breakfast, I fixed a plate for me and Kendra and I was about to pour us a glass of orange juice when my cell phone rang. I answered it.

"Miranda, we have a problem. I went over our accounts this morning and I noticed that all the scholarship money is gone." Crystal informed me.

"What do you mean it's gone? How can that be?" I asked in disbelief. Just when things were starting to look up for me something else happened.

"I have no idea."

"Okay, I'm on my way." I said. I called Kendra down for breakfast and told her I had to leave the house and then I left and drove to my organization.

When I went arrived, I sprinted in the building and went to Crystal's office. Crystal was staring at her computer screen in disbelief.

"Come here and take a look at this." She said.

I walked around the desk and looked at the computer screen and sure enough the balance was zero dollars. "This just doesn't make any sense. The only two people who have access to the money is me and you, and I know I didn't take it."

Crystal turned around to look at me in shock. "Are you trying to say I did this?"

"Well who else could have did this? I know I sure didn't." I didn't like having to accuse my best friend, but who else could have taken it.

"Maybe it was a hacker or something, I don't know." Crystal suggested.

I smacked my lips. "That's the first thing people say when they have been caught doing something online. They try to blame it on a hacker, but I just don't believe this, and until I find this money I have no other choice but to fire you." I said and then walked around the desk and stood in front of her.

Crystal looked at me in disbelief and I knew how she felt because I was in disbelief too, but I had to do what needed to be done. This money was important to these young ladies.

"I can't believe you would accuse me of something like this, but you know what." Crystal said and went into her purse and pulled out her checkbook and tore off a check and began filling it out. "Here, this is a check for two hundred thousand dollars to replace the scholarship money. That's more than half of my savings gone, but I don't want to see the young lady we choose miss out on this scholarship money." Crystal stood up. "You know I really thought you were my friend but I see that you are not." Crystal left and came back with a couple of boxes and started packing up her things.

I just watched her in silence as she finished packing up her things and then left. I picked up the check she had written and stared at it wondering if I had made a mistake, but if she didn't take the money than who did?

CHAPTER 28

Nathan

I was distracted most of the day at work thinking about how I was going to replace the money, but I managed to get through half of my surgeries with no problem. I was about to take my break, and I didn't want to eat in the cafeteria because I really didn't feel like being around anyone, so I got my food and took it back to the attending's lounge.

I sat down and got comfortable on the couch and was just about to take a bite out of my sandwich when Leah came in with her lunch. "You seemed down all day and I wanted to keep you company." She said and sat down next to me.

"I am. I took money from my wife's organization that she gives away to young ladies who deserve and need scholarships."

"Nathan, how could you?" Leah asked in shock.

I shook my head. "I was desperate." I told her.

"You need to replace that money quick, and I think I might have the perfect solution."

"What is it?" I asked desperately.

Leah hesitated for a moment and then said. "I used to have a thing going on with Harry?"

I raised my eyebrow. "What kind of thing?" I asked not liking what I was hearing.

"Do you really want details?"

"No, go on."

"He has a private room in the back of the club and I was back there drinking with him, and I watched him go in the safe and he has a lot of money in the safe. Probably millions, and I remembered the combination he put in. I have a good memory."

"What are you suggesting?" I asked afraid of what she was about to say.

"I have a cousin who is a hacker and he can disable the alarm system at the lounge and you can go in and get the money out of his safe without him knowing. It's so much money in there that he probably won't notice it's missing."

I sighed heavily. "I don't know about this Leah. This sounds too risky and dangerous."

"I know. Harry and George are two people you won't want to mess with. I heard they chopped off the fingers of a guy that didn't pay them back a loan, but they won't know it was us who did it. What other choice do you have?"

She was right I didn't have much of a choice, and if I could take money from my own wife then I guess I could take money from them. "Okay when can we do this?"

"Let's do this tomorrow, but my cousin will probably want a cut of the money, so we can just take a little extra for him."

"Okay." I agreed trying to ignore the sinking feeling in my stomach.

CHAPTER 29

Nathan

It was three days later, and Leah and I had the whole plan laid out. I had met with Leah's cousin Elliot who was an average looking guy in his early twenties. He explained to us that he could only disable the alarm system for ten minutes, so we had to get in and get out quickly. He also gave me something to pick the lock with and that made me curious about what else he was into.

It was 2:30 in the morning and the three of us was sitting in the empty parking lot in front of the lounge. There was not much traffic coming by at this hour so I wasn't that worried about someone seeing us. My heart was racing fast but I knew I had to do this especially after Miranda told me that she fired Crystal for taking the money. I didn't think she would notice the money was missing this soon. So, I had to replace that money quickly, so she could fix her friendship with Crystal.

"Are you ready?" Leah asked.

"No, but I'm going to do this anyway. I really don't think you should go in with me. You should just wait in the car with your cousin." I didn't know what could go wrong so I didn't want her in harms way if something did.

"Nonsense, I'm not going to let you do this by yourself."

I stared at her and saw the determined look on her face and I knew she wasn't changing her mind. "Okay, but why don't you just wait out front."

"No, she shouldn't wait out front because that will seem suspicious if someone happens to drive by. I think you should wait in the car and call Nathan on his cell phone if something doesn't look right." Elliot suggested.

"That makes sense." Leah reluctantly agreed.

"I'm about to disable the alarm system, so as soon as I do that you need to quickly go in and come back out in ten minutes." Elliot told me.

I nodded my head.

I watched Elliot as he tapped some keys on his laptop then he said. "Okay, go now."

I quickly got out of the car with the bag to put the money in and went up to the door and I hesitated a moment before picking the lock because I was afraid that the alarm would still go off. But I shook the fear off because I knew I didn't have time to waste and I carefully picked the lock and opened the door. I went inside and paused expecting someone to come around the corner.

When no one came I went around back behind the bar and around the corner where the private room was just like Leah said. I thought I was going to have to pick that lock but the door opened with no problem and I went into the room. It was a nicely furnished cozy room, and I spotted the safe at the back of the room and darted towards it. I used the combination Leah gave me and the safe popped open and my mouth went wide when I saw how much money was in the safe. They were wrapped neatly in rubber bands.

I pulled out a stack and notice it was filled with hundreds. And I estimated that it was about twenty thousand a stack, so I took more than what I needed and put the money inside the bag and quickly exited the room and the lounge. I made sure I locked the door behind me and ran to the car. My adrenaline was pumping so hard.

"Good time, it took you five minutes." Elliot said.

I didn't say anything I just left the parking lot as fast as I could and went back to Leah's house where were we gave Elliot his cut and there was still extra money left over after I had the money I needed to replace Tim's scholarship money and Miranda's organization money. We split the remaining money, and I thanked Elliot and he left with a smile on his face from his new fortune.

I spend the night with Leah because I had told Miranda I that I was working all night at the hospital. Instead of having sex that night Leah and I just held each other. I felt relieved and the first thing in the morning I was going to replace all the money and finally my life could get back to normal.

CHAPTER 30

Miranda   '

It was a Saturday morning and I was spending the day with Tim. Nathan was at work and Kendra had spend the night at Shannon's house. I had been feeling down all week because of what happened with Crystal. I had a feeling I was wrong, and that feeling was confirmed when I checked the account again and the money was there. It was the strangest thing and I wondered if it was some kind of glitch in the banking system. I immediately called Crystal to apologize but she wouldn't answer my calls. I even stopped by her house and she didn't even come to the door and I knew she was home because I saw her car parked in the drive-way. I wasn't going to give up because I felt like eventually we would repair our friendship.

I was going to treat Tim to a day of shopping because he would be graduating next month, and I was so proud of him. He was going to be the salutatorian of his class. That was one step behind the valedictorian, and I was very excited about his future.

I took Tim to all the expensive stores and he complained that I was spending too much money on him, but he deserved all that and much more. After we finished shopping we had a nice lunch and Tim and I talked about everything. He told me how much he loved his girlfriend Brandy and that he was going to propose to her right after college, and I told him that I support him as long as it didn't distract him from his work and he assured me that it wouldn't.

The House Always Wins   Shanika Roach

After lunch we headed home. I was going to take a nap and Tim had plans to go out with Brandy later. When we arrived home, I unlocked the door and Tim and I walked inside the house. I locked the door behind us and Tim was right in front of me as soon as he walked past the foyer someone came around the corner and hit him over the head. I watched as Tim feel to the floor and I screamed, but my screaming quickly stopped when I felt something heavy crash into my head and then there was darkness.

CHAPTER 31

Nathan

After doing two surgeries I told the chief of surgery that I was going to head home for today. I was so relieved that all the money was replaced in the accounts and I wanted to spend some extra time with my family.

When I arrived home, I opened the door and closed it behind me and when I went into the living room nothing could have prepared me for what I saw. Tim and Miranda were both tied to our kitchen chairs with duck-tape over their mouths. I was about to rush over to them when Harry and George came out of the kitchen both holding guns and I knew that my chickens had come home to roost.

"I'm glad you finally made it home, Nathan, because we've been waiting for you to join the party." Harry said with a menacing look on his face.

"Please let my family go." I pleaded. I looked over at Tim and Miranda and they had scared looks on their faces and tears were streaming down Miranda's face.

"I can't do that. You took something from us." George said.

"I asked your family about the money, but it seems that you've kept them in the dark about your gambling and your girlfriend Leah." Harry said and laughed.

I looked at Miranda with a look of regret on my face. I never wanted her to find out about Leah especially not like this.

"I know you're probably wondering how I know where you lived. Well Leah told me. You see George went to deposit money in the safe and he noticed some money was missing so we looked at the security tapes and he who do we see opening our safe?" Harry asked.

I didn't say anything. I just stared at him. I was scared out of my mind and couldn't believe that I didn't think about the possibility of them having cameras in the place.

"I was surprised to see you stealing from me and I knew that only one person could have told you about it. So, we went to pay Leah a little visit and after knocking her around a little bit she told us where you lived. I couldn't believe you would steal from me." Harry said.

"I'm sorry." I said.

"Not as sorry as you're going to be." Harry said and George left the living room and came back with another one of our kitchen chairs and some ropes and tape.

"Now sit down in the chair." Harry said and pointed the gun at me.

I hesitated for a moment. I knew if I sat in the chair that our chances of getting out of this alive would be slim to none.

Harry walked over to Miranda and pointed the gun at her head and Miranda began to cry harder. "Don't even thinking about doing anything stupid Doc."

I knew I had no other choice and I certainly was not going to risk him killing my wife, so I reluctantly sat in the chair and let George tie me up.

Harry walked over to me. "You see this isn't about the money, it's about the principle of the thing. See we liked you Doc, and if you had came to us and told us you were in trouble we would have more than likely helped you out. Leah told us all about you losing your son's college tuition and taking money from your wife's organization. I saw the look of shock pass over Miranda and Tim's faces.

"See instead of you paying us our money back we're going to hit you were it really hurts." Harry said and George walked over to Miranda and started punching her.

"Leave her alone!" I shouted. I watched helplessly as he punched her until she was finally unconscious.

"Lower you voice, we wouldn't want to alert you neighbors." Harry said.

And then I watched in horror as George walked over to Tim and pointed the gun at him, and my heart began to pound violently in my chest. "No, please don't hurt my son. I'll give you all the money in my accounts!" I yelled out.

Harry laughed at me. "At the lounge you always bragged about your son and how proud of him you are, so it would be ashamed if something happened to him because of you."

"Please don't." I begged.

"We're just playing with you Doc, you didn't think we were that bad, did you?" George said and took the gun off of Tim and started walking towards me.

I breathed a sigh of relief, but that relief was quickly taken away when George turned around and shot Tim twice and I yelled out as I saw the blood pouring from Tim's body. Harry silenced me by punching me in the face. I didn't care what he did to me now. With my son gone he could kill me too. George disappeared in the kitchen and came out with a hammer and walked towards me and handed the hammer to Harry. I knew Leah warned me that Harry and George were not to be played with, but I had no idea they would react this way.

"We're not finish with you yet Doc. See you're a surgeon so you need your hands. So, I'm about to teach you a very important lesson. The house always wins, and when you cheat the house there is a high price to pay." Harry said as he began to beat both of my hands with the hammer.

I was in so much pain that I eventually passed out.

CHAPTER 32

Miranda

Three years later

Nathan and I were now divorced. I suffered from a broken jaw, nose and I had a concussion after the beating I took, but I still attended my son's funeral. It was a huge turnout at his funeral. Everyone was so sad that his life was tragically cut short when he had such a promising future. There was no way I could stay married to Nathan after he got our son killed. The cheating I could have forgiven. I received half of Nathan's money in the divorce settlement, but I didn't really need it because my parents set up a trust fund for me that I never touched. I was saving it for a rainy day and Nathan never knew about it. I lived in a nice two-story three-bedroom house, there was no way I could go back in live in the house my son was murdered in. Kendra was now in college and lived on campus and our relationship was better than before. I was glad she wasn't home when that terrible incident happened because she had already been through enough. She had finally forgiven me for making her have that abortion. She missed her brother terribly and so did I. I started a college fund in Tim's name to be given to a male and I still had the other to be given to a female, and Crystal was back working for my organization.

After learning of Tim's death Crystal immediately came to be by my side and she quickly forgave me when I explained everything that went on. She said she couldn't believe that Nathan had gotten caught up in gambling and neither did I, but I knew something was wrong and I chose to ignore it. Maybe if I had paid more attention I could have gotten him some help before it got this out of hand. But there was nothing I could about it now. David and I were still friends and we talked from time to time but that was about it because my family was my main focus.

There was another huge surprise. A few months after Tim's death Brandy came by to tell me she was pregnant. She said she found out she was pregnant right after the funeral, but she wasn't ready to tell me yet. She gave birth to a beautiful healthy boy that she named Timothy Jr, and he looked just like Timothy eyes and all. It brought me comfort that I had some piece of my son left and Brandy attended college in Arizona and me and her parents helped her out. My life is a little better now, but it will never be the same without Tim, but I'm leaning on God even harder these days and I know with God by my side, I will make it.

CHAPTER 33

Nathan

Three years later

My life had changed tremendously over the last three years.
Right after Harry and George tragically hurt me and my family the
police came in right when they tried to leave. Apparently, Leah
felt guilty about telling them where I lived, so she called the police
and told them they needed to come to my house immediately, but I
wish she would have called them sooner. Harry and George are
now in jail serving life sentences where they belong. They didn't
even bother with a trial they just pleaded guilty. They were caught
red handed after all. I'm thankful that my family didn't have to be
put through a trial. Of course, after everything that happened Leah
and I didn't continue to see each other.

After Tim's funeral I went to numerous orthopedic surgeons
until I found one that could help me. I had numerous surgeries and
bone grafts and finally I had full use of my hands again, but they
went numb sometimes, so I wasn't cleared for surgery yet. The
surgeon told me that the numbness could go away over time. It
hurt that I couldn't do the thing that God had blessed me with, but
I still taught classes at the hospital.

Losing my son and my wife leaving me caused me to take a real
hard look at my life. I had always been overwhelmed with the
responsibility of taking care of my family since I was a teenager
and it got worse once I became an adult, and surgery was the one

thing I never failed at, so when I finally failed at a surgery I didn't know how to handle it. Instead of relying on God I chose to gamble, and it slowly got out of control, and it cost me everything. After what happened I had no desire to gamble anymore. I still wondered why Tim had to die in all of this. I really would have rather it been me. I often questioned God about it, but I know that there are some things you won't get the answers to on this earth. I can't sleep at night thinking about the wonderful future Tim could have had and I just hope I get to see him again when I go over to the other side. Miranda still hasn't fully forgiven me, but she's cordial to me at best and Kendra is the same way towards me. I just hope they can fully forgive me some day. I do get to see my grandson sometimes and that brings me joy. It's like seeing Tim grow up all over again. Shelia and I's relationship was back on track. I couldn't judge her after all the things I have done. We even visited our mother together. Most visits she didn't know who we were, but it still felt good just to see her.

I often think about Harry's words about the house always wins and he was right. The house always wins, but I was focusing on the wrong house. I should have focused on the House of the Lord, the house that has already won and will continue to win.

.

Made in the USA
Coppell, TX
02 April 2021